"So you [...] guy with [...]" *he asked disdainfully....*

"No. I intend to catch him with my sparkling personality, my scintillating wit, my impeccable good breeding and homemaking skills, to name just a few. I'm just saying that once he's good and caught he won't suffer."

The whole world was just plain off kilter. His best buddy Rick's baby sister simply shouldn't be talking like this. Sure, she was chronologically old enough and everything, but it was just wrong for him to be here in her kitchen talking about kissing and sexual stuff. Plain wrong...

Dear Reader,

Have you started your spring cleaning yet? If not, we have a great motivational plan: For each chore you complete, reward yourself with one Silhouette Romance title! And with the standout selection we have this month, you'll be finished reorganizing closets, steaming carpets and cleaning behind the refrigerator in record time!

Take a much-deserved break with the exciting new ROYALLY WED: THE MISSING HEIR title, *In Pursuit of a Princess*, by Donna Clayton. The search for the missing St. Michel heir leads an undercover princess straight into the arms of a charming prince. Then escape with Diane Pershing's SOULMATES addition, *Cassie's Cowboy*. Could the dreamy hero from her daughter's bedtime stories be for real?

Lugged out and wiped down the patio furniture? Then you deserve a double treat with Cara Colter's *What Child Is This?* and Belinda Barnes's *Daddy's Double Due Date*. In Colter's tender tearjerker, a tiny stranger reunites a couple torn apart by tragedy. And in Barnes's warm romance, a bachelor who isn't the "cootchie-coo" type discovers he's about to have twins!

You're almost there! Once you've rounded up every last dust bunny, you're really going to need some fun. In Terry Essig's *Before You Get to Baby...* and Sharon De Vita's *A Family To Be*, childhood friends discover that love was always right next door. De Vita's series, SADDLE FALLS, moves back to Special Edition next month.

Even if you skip the spring cleaning this year, we hope you don't miss our books. We promise, this is one project you'll love doing.

Happy reading!

Mary-Theresa Hussey

Mary-Theresa Hussey
Senior Editor

Please address questions and book requests to:
Silhouette Reader Service
U.S.: 3010 Walden Ave., P.O. Box 1325, Buffalo, NY 14269
Canadian: P.O. Box 609, Fort Erie, Ont. L2A 5X3

Before You Get to Baby...

TERRY ESSIG

SILHOUETTE *Romance*®

Published by Silhouette Books

America's Publisher of Contemporary Romance

For my daughter Andrea whose childhood
watery wedding fantasy still makes us laugh,
and my niece Betsy for all the wetland information.
May your princes be charming, your dreams reality.
And, Andrea, may your barge never sink.

 SILHOUETTE BOOKS

ISBN 0-373-19583-4

BEFORE YOU GET TO BABY…

Copyright © 2002 by Mary Therese Essig

Books by Terry Essig

Silhouette Romance

House Calls #552
The Wedding March #662
Fearless Father #725
Housemates #1015
Hardheaded Woman #1044
Daddy on Board #1114
Mad for the Dad #1198
What the Nursery Needs... #1272
The Baby Magnet #1435
A Gleam in His Eye #1472
Before You Get to Baby... #1583

Silhouette Special Edition

Father of the Brood #796

TERRY ESSIG

says that writing is her escape valve from a life that leaves little time for recreation or hobbies. With a husband and six young children, Terry works on her stories a little at a time, between seeing to her children's piano, sax and trombone lessons, their gymnastics, ice skating and swim team practices, and her own activities of leading a Brownie troop, participating in a car pool and attending organic chemistry classes. Her ideas, she says, come from her imagination and her life—neither one of which is lacking!

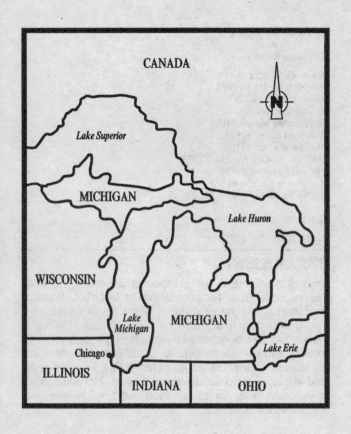

Chapter One

"Sex."

"Excuse me?"

"Well, ideally it should be *good* sex."

"*That's* what you think a guy is looking for most in a relationship?" Mary Frances Parker looked with barely concealed horror at her brother's best friend. Clearly, Drew Wiseman was not the man she should be going to for tips on what a man looks for in a woman. "Sex? That's *it?*"

"Like I said, good sex, not just any sex," Drew continued, oblivious to her discomfort. "I mean, quantity counts and everything but quality should play a definite role here."

"That is so totally ridiculous. I wish you could hear yourself."

"Hey, you're the one who came ringing my doorbell wanting to know the guy's perspective without so much as a hello first. I'm just being honest."

Frannie thought of her brother, due to be married in a month's time. "So what you're basically saying here is that Rick was ruled by nothing but hormones when he proposed to Evie? My friend Betsy's mind and personality had nothing to do with Tom's proposal? Sheesh. Men are so pathetic. I'm starting to wonder why I want to find one to marry in the first place."

Her words threw Drew for a loop. Married? Frannie? Why, she was just a kid. Had he known she was in the market he'd have tailored his advice. After all, the idea of Frannie providing what every man looked for in a relationship disturbed him for reasons he didn't want to explore. "So if we're so pathetic and all, why aren't you busy thinking up ways to avoid us? I mean, why would you want to bind yourself to one of us for the rest of your life anyway?"

"God only knows." Using the tip of her index finger Frannie glumly picked up cookie crumbs from the kitchen table where she'd made herself at home. "I keep thinking they can't possibly all be as shallow as they appear, and I do want to have a family and children." She shrugged. "Lord knows, with my brothers, I've picked up enough boxer shorts dropped within spitting distance of a clothes hamper and fished enough dirty socks out from under beds to last me a lifetime, but the plain truth of the matter is men are a necessity if you want a family and babies," she pointed out, sounding almost forlorn.

Drew sat back in his chair. Would he ever understand women? "Next you're going to tell me your biological clock is ticking. Am I right?" He rolled his eyes in anticipation of her answer. Andrew couldn't understand it. His friends' biological alarms seemed to be going off in depressingly large numbers lately. Didn't anybody get that babies were a pain? They upchucked, and they did disgusting things in their pants. They got up in the middle of the night, for God's sake, the middle of the night.

"Well, it is," his best friend's little sister answered defensively.

"So let it tick, Frannie," Andrew advised. "I mean,

come on, it's not like you've got one foot in the grave."
He shrugged. Drew was five years older than Frannie. He
certainly didn't feel an uncontrollable need to nest. "The
world is overpopulated anyway. If you need to hear the
pitter-patter of little feet all that bad, get a dog. They'll
drool, throw up and piddle on the carpeting same as any
baby."

Frannie glowered. "I wouldn't expect you to understand."

"So why'd you ask?"

"Because you're safe."

No man liked to hear himself described as safe. "What's
that supposed to mean?" Safe? He wasn't safe. He was
lean and mean. Andrew had done time in the military. Why,
he could easily produce a dozen or more guys who'd be
happy to testify just how mean he could be. *Safe*. What was
that? He never should have let Frannie in the door. The
fact she'd shown up with a plate of her homemade cookies
should have been an indication she was up to no good.
When would he ever learn that there was no such thing as
a free meal, or in this case, free cookie?

And look at this. Frannie'd been there all of ten minutes
and sure enough, here he was getting all worked up. Frannie could rile him the way nobody else ever had, or in all
likelihood, ever could.

Frannie sighed. "Well, it certainly wasn't meant as an
insult. Look, all I meant was that I can't ask somebody
who's a potential mate, now can I? They'd run the opposite
direction if they thought I was actively looking for a
spouse. Why are men so paranoid?"

"We're not paranoid, we're realistic. Women *are* out to
get us." Drew waved an arm out in the air. "Look at Rick.
And our buddy Phil. Then let's not forget Nate Bowman."
He threw up the other hand. "There goes Wednesday bowl-
ing, Friday night poker *and* the occasional drive into Chi-

cago to see the White Sox play. *They're* all too busy out
picking china patterns. Meanwhile, what am *I* supposed to
do for entertainment, hmm? None of these women stop to
think about their guys' guy relationships, do they? What is
it with your sex and this commitment thing you've all got?
Why can't you ladies be happy without a picket fence
around your tidy Cape Cod and your two-point-three pre-
cocious children?''

Drew picked up his beer and took a thirsty slug. He
wasn't positive, but he was pretty sure Frannie had just
insulted him. He knew he shouldn't ask, but it just showed
how wrong she was and how on the edge he liked to live.
''And just why am I safe from your machinations I'd like
to know?'' Not that he wanted to be the target of all that
fire power. Of course he didn't.

''Well, for one thing I couldn't possibly live with someone who liked country and western.'' Frannie bit back a
laugh as Drew gaped at her. Then, restlessly, she drummed
her fingers on the tabletop. ''Okay, while it's true I loathe
and despise country, there's a little more to it than just your
pitiable taste in music. A woman looks for something different in a husband than a date,'' she explained carefully,
thinking as she spoke. Teasing Drew was fun, but if she
intended to pick his brain, which she did, he deserved to
know she'd thought this thing through. It wasn't just a
whim on her part. Besides, there was no harm in letting
him know she'd be off the market before too much longer.
Frannie scowled. As if he'd care. *Why* couldn't he care?
Everything would be so much easier.

Right away, Drew knew Frannie was actually serious
about this current craziness. Frannie never thought before
she spoke. Whatever entered her brain exited her mouth.
Oh, man, he was going to have to talk to her brother Rick
about this.

''For a mate, she needs somebody steady, reliable. Someone who'll take out the trash and be able to find the clothes hamper when he undresses at night. Somebody who'll walk the floors with her when the baby has colic. Someone who actually replaces the toilet paper—on the holder, not just sets it in the near vicinity—when he finishes off a roll.''

By God, he *was* insulted. He could do all those things. If he wanted. It was hardly *his* fault his toilet paper holder had come away from the wall a month or so ago and he'd been too busy to fix it, now was it? What else could he do but set the roll on the floor? Anyone could see that.

Drew couldn't believe he was even having this conversation. Damn it, nobody ignited his fuse the way Frannie did. Didn't the woman understand that the easiest way to handle colic was to not have the baby in the first place?

"Somebody you don't mind sharing your genetic code with, you know? Everybody I know is out there sharing their genetic code. I'm telling you, every close friend I have is either married or will be by the end of the summer. You should see Sue Ellen's little boy. He's just too cute. I want one of those, Drew, I really do. The thing is, it took Sue Ellen three years to get pregnant, and she got married right out of college. You know, a man starts losing some of his potency once he hits his mid twenties, I figured I ought to get on the stick and find somebody now."

"I may be twenty-nine but I'm quite sure I wouldn't have any trouble at all impregnating anything needing impregnating," Drew growled. "In fact it's been my greatest fear. It's why we men are so darn careful. I never wanted to have to pay the price for thinking with my gonads."

Frannie ignored him. "I also want somebody who's intelligent. And I wouldn't mind decent-looking, either. I've given up on Mel Gibson coming to his senses, but surely decent-looking isn't asking too much." She grimaced. "Call me shallow, but I don't want any frog-faced children. Breakfast is too early in the morning to have to face am-

phibians across the table. I'm on the short side, so in order
to compensate, I'm thinking tall, too. No point in the boys
being shrimpsters if I can help it. Mom always said it was
as easy to fall in love with a rich man as a poor one, but I
don't really care all that much about money. I don't mind
pulling my fair share and contributing to the family income.
But if you extrapolate a little bit here, and the playing field
being equal in other ways, I mean between two guys, both
being intelligent, decent-looking and now that I think about
it, neither one an early balder, it should be as easy to fall
for the tall guy as the short one, don't you think?''

Drew shook his head in despair as he tried to figure out
the logic behind that bit of nonsense. Near as he could tell,
he'd been insulted. Again. She might be his best friend's
little sister and as cute as a button, but she'd crossed the
line. There was not a damn thing wrong with his genetic
code. Not a damn thing. He had an engineering degree from
Purdue University, didn't he? You didn't get that with peas
for brain, now did you?

And more than one woman had come on to him during
the eleven years since high school. There was a small cadre
of females out there who'd rate his looks higher than dog
meat, Andrew thought more than a bit defensively even as
he rubbed the nose that had been broken a dozen years back
when he'd taken a hockey puck in the face. It might be a
little crooked, but hey, if a woman expected perfection,
she'd have to provide it herself. He knew for a fact Frannie
had a scar down one arm from the surgery it had taken to
put her arm back together after an attempt to go around the
moon on the playground swing set years ago. Man, he'd
almost had heart failure that day. He and Rick had been
baby-sitting Frannie when she'd tried that little trick. Rick
had accused a wailing Frannie of doing it on purpose just
to get them in trouble. It hadn't been the first time. Or the

last. And here she was, back at it again, obviously determined to draw him into this latest batch of nuttiness.

But he digressed. He was intelligent and decent-looking. Hadn't Debi...Dulci...whoever, gotten all rhapsodic over his eyes? Like she'd never seen the color blue before. Drew almost snorted. Go figure. It was a simple factor of genetics. His mother had blue eyes, his father's eyes were brown, but he obviously carried a recessive gene for blue. Drew had just as obviously gotten it. Simple. No big deal. Try telling that to Deirdre. Yeah, that was it, Deirdre.

At least he *had* an eye color. Frannie's license said brown, but that was only because they had to fit her into a category. *Her* eyes were this oddball color only a woman would have a name for—toffee, toast or maybe café au lait. Drew rolled his eyes. Who thought up these names anyway? he thought with a sneer. And that was just the inside part of her iris. Then there was this darker band around the edge. Dark chocolate bark or something. Whatever.

And furthermore, even though scrupulous honesty would have him admitting that he might have just missed making the six-foot mark, any engineer in the world would tell you that a small margin of error was allowable and you'd still meet specs. At five eleven and three-quarters he was six foot plus or minus a quarter of an inch, so he claimed six feet. Totally within code and definitely un-short.

A growl built up in his throat. "Seems to me you're asking for an awful lot. What's the guy going to get in return? Who's going to marry a little bit like you? A man wants a woman he doesn't have to worry about losing in the sheets at night. An armful, you know? Something it would take more than a spring zephyr to blow away."

"I am not that little," Frannie responded stiffly.

Ah, so she could dish it out, but couldn't take it.

"And there you go again," she added. "Is sex all you think about?"

"Me and my half of the world's population. Yeah, pretty much."

Frustration rang in Frannie's voice. "Don't you want someone who can create a home? Do you ever worry about character, personality, intelligence, humor, for God's sake? Don't you want to share a good laugh with a woman you care about?"

"Not when I'm in bed with her," Drew fervently assured Frannie.

Frannie threw up her hands in exasperation. "Oh, for crying out loud." She rose and snatched up the plate of cookies she'd brought as a bribe.

"Hey!" Drew protested.

Frannie didn't relent. "Nothing deeper than surface appeal matters to you," she said. "You just said so. You couldn't possibly care that I also bake the best oatmeal cookies in a three-state radius."

"Food is another basic need, right up there with sex. A man's got to keep his strength up, after all. And they're okay," Drew allowed, not wanting to feed her ego. She gave him enough of a hard time as it was. "Even if they do have raisins in them. It would be too bad if they went to waste."

"I'll freeze them. Take them in my lunch."

"All right, all right. I'm sorry, already. Put the cookies back and we'll talk. Sheesh. Women are so sensitive."

"We are not." Frannie hesitated, then reluctantly sat back down. She kept the cookies in front of her, her arms curled protectively around the plate. "So come on now, Drew, give. Seriously, what's a guy looking for when he's ready to settle down?"

Drew squirmed uncomfortably in his chair. The topic had him on edge. "Look, Frannie, every guy is different in what they find attractive in a woman. Just like every woman is different. Didn't I hear you telling Rick the other day that your friend Annie was wasting her time on some dweeb? That you couldn't figure out what she saw in the guy?''

Frannie thought. Okay, he had a point, but it wasn't enough to get her to release the cookies. She wanted some guidelines here, not a cop-out. ''All right, so *generally speaking* what's likely to interest a guy enough to get him to the altar?'' Meanly, she picked up a cookie and waved it in the air a couple of times before nibbling delicately at the brown edge.

Damn her, Frannie knew him too well. Drew shifted uncomfortably once more. For most of the past fifteen years, ever since Drew's family had moved to St. Joseph, Michigan, Andrew and Rick had been inseparable. Five years younger than her next oldest sibling, Frannie was obviously the family's much-adored bonus baby. He and Rick had baby-sat Frannie too many times to count. They'd driven her to piano lessons, softball and dance. Drew had helplessly patted her back while she'd cried on Rick's shoulder after the break-up with her first boyfriend and uselessly assured her the jerk hadn't been good enough for her. Heck, he'd marked the seasons by the color of the rubber bands she'd picked for her braces each month at the orthodontist. Red and green in December which made her look like her teeth were growing moss, but better than the orange and black she'd favored in October.

In all that time he'd spent watching her grow, Drew had never once realized that she'd been watching him as well. The little brat knew the edges were his favorite part. Just look at her savoring *his* edge.

Drew would have to be under particularly diabolical torture before he'd admit that her cookies were, in fact, the best in town even if they did have raisins. Heck, they'd have to stake him to an anthill and disassemble his remote control before his very eyes. The problem was, he'd only had a handful before Frannie'd gone into her snit. Previous to that it had been a long dry spell of nothing but store-bought. The injustice of it sang through him. Drew wracked his brain for something Frannie would consider worthy.

"Okay," Drew finally said. "I'll tell you what. Leave the cookies here. Brain food, you know, and I'll think about it. I'll come over to dinner some time in the next few weeks and we'll talk." He raised a hopeful eyebrow.

Frannie eyed him with disgust. Man, Drew gave her no credit at all. He still thought of her as a gullible twelve-year-old who'd fall for the old Tom Sawyer's I'm-having-such-fun-whitewashing-this-fence-but-if-you-pay-me-enough-I-might-let-you-do-it-instead gambit. He and Rick had used that ruse whenever her mom had assigned them a task to be done while they baby-sat her. Pitiful. Absolutely pitiful. She crossed her arms over her chest.

"Half a dozen cookies now, the rest on delivery of the goods, no later than this weekend or the deal's off. And I'm not cooking for you. I'll pay my own way, but we're going out."

Damn, but she was a tough little negotiator. You had to respect that about her. He and Rick had taught her well with all their stupid pranks. He had nobody to blame for this but himself. "You want to talk about this in a restaurant? Where anybody and their brother can listen in? You know how close tables are in those places."

Frannie thought about that and nodded. "All right, I'll cook. In fact, we'll grill. You bring the steaks and the wine. I'll do the salad, bread and dessert."

Drew scowled. Evidently he wasn't as smart as he thought he was. He also suspected it was probably the best deal he was going to get, so he nodded his head in agreement. "Okay. I'll get back to you when I've...what?" Frannie was vehemently shaking her head and frowning.

"This Friday. My place. Seven o'clock."

"Frannie," he explained patiently, "This Friday is part

of March Madness. Intercollegiate basketball play-offs, you know? Rick made me kick money into a pool thing he started. Frankly, I don't think Villanova can do it, but it was all there was left and you never know so I...now what?''

"No excuses. This Friday, seven o'clock, or no cookies. If you're good maybe I'll let you check the score once or twice.''

"Man, you're a pain." But Drew really, really wanted those cookies. He was a scientist. He'd taken several different types of chemistry. He still had lab nightmares all these years later. One thing Drew knew for sure, he could weigh and measure with the best of them. But when he attempted cookies, no matter how carefully Drew doled out the ingredients, they simply didn't hold a candle to Frannie's. Actually, it was a major point of frustration for him as he'd seen her in action in the kitchen. Frannie would have flunked chem lab, any science lab, that was for sure. She just sort of threw things together. And whatever it was always turned out well. "All right, all right. This Friday. But I get a dozen cookies up front.''

"Eight.''

"Ten." Drew casually inched his hand toward the cookie plate.

Frannie cradled the plate more closely. "Nine." She started counting them out.

"Okay. I think I read somewhere that for attracting a mate, we're all operating on a subconscious instinctual level. We only think we've gotten civilized over the eons.''

"If you're trying to tell me men still operate on caveman level, I'm not all that surprised. I will not, however, take it kindly if one of them tries to conk me on the head and drag me home by the hair.''

Drew snorted. "You haven't got enough hair to get a good grip.''

Frannie patted her short crop of curls protectively. "Short hair is easy to take care of as well as very stylish." She sniffed disdainfully. "Shows how much you know about fashion."

"Guys like long. We don't care if it's fashionable or not." Drew gathered his booty in front of him.

Frannie covered her plate with plastic wrap and rose. "If you don't care about what's in, why is your hair so carefully mussed up today, in that bedhead style guys are so into right now?"

Drew sat back, disgusted. "You asked, I answered. Leave my hair out of it. How big is your waist?"

"My waist?"

Drew waved away her puzzled look. "Never mind. We'll get into it come Friday." If he couldn't get any more cookies out of her right now, he wasn't going to waste his ammunition.

"What about my waist?" Frannie wanted to know.

"Friday," Drew reiterated and shooed Frannie out the door so he could enjoy his treat in peace. Women. Go figure. Tell them what they want to know and they argue. Drew shoveled a cookie up and into his mouth feeling slightly aggrieved. Now he had to spend the next few days thinking up ways for a member of the opposite sex to trap one of his own. Talk about disloyal. He'd sold out to the enemy with barely a whimper. A handful of cookies was all it had taken. Disgusted, he crunched down hard on another one. "Well, too darned bad. They're all grown men. They can fend for themselves. If one of them gets caught, he probably deserves it for being so stupid as to fall for all those female ploys."

Frannie drove home proud of herself. She'd started the process. Subtlety was lost on a man like Drew—actually on most men, she decided as she signaled a left turn and left his street behind. You had to hit them over their hard, fat heads to get their attention. She'd done that.

"Ought to be interesting to see what he comes up with," she told herself as she turned again, right this time. Frannie came up to a red light, drummed her fingers as she waited. "At least I've got him thinking about marriage. That's something." She accelerated as the light changed. "And if he still refuses to open his eyes and see what's right in front of them, I swear I'll use whatever he tells me to find myself somebody who *will* appreciate me. See if I don't, the unappreciative bum." Frannie pulled into a spot in front of her neat little frame one-story. "And I'll tell you something else. When and if that man does wake up, he's going to have some serious making up to do. Serious making up." And she sniffed in self-righteous justification as she walked up her front walk.

Late Friday afternoon she was still sniffing at regular intervals at the male population's thick-headedness in general, one Andrew Wiseman's in particular. "Wiseman, hah!" Frannie spat as she pounded the sofa-back cushions back into shape in anticipation of his arrival. Setting the scene was important, after all. "There's a misnomer if ever there was one. Blindman is more like it. Andrew Stupid-head has a certain cachet as well." The sofa beaten into submission, Frannie surveyed the room, hands on her hips. Even if it was on a subconscious level, she wanted Drew to see the kind of home she could create.

Satisfied with the room check, she started down the short hall to her bedroom. "Obviously, I must have a very perverse nature to find the man this appealing. But I've got to make my play now before somebody else snaps him up. He's within shouting distance of thirty, for heaven's sake, he should be more than ready to settle down. I'd always planned to be the one standing in front of him when he woke up. Where the heck did that silk teddy go? Ah, there it is and my...yes, got that too.'' She headed out of the bedroom and into the bath.

''Well, I just can't wait any longer,'' Frannie said as she reached in to turn on the shower. ''His social life is too darn active and he still treats me like I'm his little sister. Not after tonight,'' she vowed as she stepped into the steaming stall. ''Not after tonight.''

Drew fidgeted out on Frannie's front stoop before he rang the bell. He checked his fly, made sure his shirt was tucked in and even checked his hair in the reflection in the front door's small inset decorative glass pane. Disgusted with himself, Drew poked the buzzer. It was just Frannie, for God's sake. Still, for some odd reason he'd felt compelled to go home after work for a quick shower, his best jeans and a clean shirt. When he'd stopped at the supermarket to pick up the steaks he'd had the most inexplicable, ridiculous urge to pick up a bunch of flowers. Now what had that been all about?

Drew shook his head as Frannie opened the door. A couple of the guys at work had been passing around some kind of bug. Maybe he was coming down with it. That could be why he felt so weird, couldn't it? Look at Frannie, she hadn't fussed, for God's sake. She was covered from neck to below her knees in some kind of voluminous apron thing. ''I don't think I've ever seen you wear an apron before,'' he said as he dubiously studied the object. She was all but drowning in yards of fabric but then again, she was a little bit of a thing.

''I had a conference with a parent after school,'' Frannie blatantly lied. All was fair in love and war, after all. Not only had there been no conference, she'd never have worn the tight, short skirt hiding under the apron to school at all. She taught second grade. If Drew thought about it once he got a gander, he'd realize that with all the floor work she did with such young children any kind of skirt, let alone this abbreviated version, would be fairly impractical. But Drew's thoughts rarely ran along the mundane or everyday practicalities of living. If it didn't have to do with recycling sludge, it got no more than cursory notice. She figured she was safe. "I didn't have time to change from my good clothes if we were going to eat on time, and I do have a tendency to be a bit messy in the kitchen." Truth was, she'd put the skimpy hug-your-rear thing on just to bother Drew.

Frannie was sloppy when she baked. He'd have hated her for a lab partner, true enough, even though her product was worth the mess. It was a logical explanation and Drew nodded. Then Frannie turned around and walked in front of him. Holy cow! Thank God he was still holding the beer he'd bought instead of drinking it, Drew thought. He'd have choked for sure. He sputtered anyway. "Uh, it was a conference with a mother, right?"

"Hmm?" Frannie rolled her hips even more with her next step. The contrast between the loose apron and the peeks he got at her snugly encased rear with each step she took had been carefully checked for effect in the mirror. She hoped he swallowed his tongue. Look at him standing there in those tight jeans and that white knit shirt with the camel-colored stripe right across his pecs. He'd done that on purpose. Everybody knew light colors made you look bigger and that horizontal strip was nothing but a blatant attempt to draw attention to the breadth of his chest. Well she'd noticed. A long time ago, she'd noticed. Frannie wasn't the slow one here.

"What is that thing supposed to be under there, a skirt? It's missing the whole bottom half if it is." He stared at her butt and cleared his throat. "A mother conference, right? Not a father conference?" Drew inhaled much-needed oxygen. "They let you wear stuff like that around little kids? Oh, boy."

"Drew, this skirt is no shorter than a pair of shorts and you've seen me in those before. Surely you knew I had legs."

"Well, yeah, but…" He gave up.

Dinner was eaten in a not-quite-companionable silence. Drew was on edge, like he was on a first date or something, but couldn't understand why. By the time dessert was produced Drew was sure he was coming down with something. He'd been feeling hot ever since Frannie had finished fussing in the kitchen and taken off the apron thing. Of course, Frannie had had him going in and out of the cold grilling the damn steaks and everybody—other than Frannie evidently—knew that wasn't good for you. He tried to remember if he'd ever seen her dressed up before. Frannie tended to live in jeans or shorts and an oversize T-shirt. But surely, in all those years, there must have been some other occasion when she'd gussied herself up when he'd been around.

Eighth-grade graduation, Drew remembered. A white dress with a big sash and daisies in her hair.

Frannie's body had changed since eighth grade. Big time, it had changed.

Andrew had sighed in relief when he'd seated her. The table hid that cute little rear he'd had no idea she had. But his relief was short-lived. Taking the chair across the small table from Frannie he was faced with her, um, Frannie's um…well, chest.

And what a fine chest it was. Nicely delineated and showcased by a snug, thinly knit sweater. Drew had a hard time not staring. Surely *that* hadn't cropped up overnight. He wasn't just getting sick. Those two handfuls had taken a while to appear. He'd evidently been out of it for quite some time if he was just noticing now that Frannie was a *woman.* Damn it, he didn't want to think of Frannie as a woman. She'd been like a sister to him for years. Suddenly he felt awkward around her. It wasn't right for him to be noticing her chest. Not right at all.

"...other night."

"Hmm? what?"

Frannie sighed and set a nice big warm chunk of gingerbread slathered with real whipped cream in front of Andrew. "Are you feeling okay, Drew? You've been in your own little world most of the night."

Drew grabbed her hand before she could retreat. "Feel my forehead, will you, Frannie? It's warm, right? I feel hot. I think I'm running a temperature."

Dutifully, Frannie felt his forehead with the back of her hand. Then, just to be mean she brushed a lock of hair back off his brow. His answering little shiver pleased her. "No, you don't feel overly warm. Must be something else. I'll check the thermostat, but I know it's set at seventy."

Drew didn't think he could stand watching her hips swing in that excuse for a skirt. "No, that's all right. I'm okay. Sit down. Let's talk."

So Frannie sat. She also deliberately leaned slightly forward and pressed her arms together. Color rose on Andrew's cheeks as cleavage popped.

He cleared his throat. "So, anyway, I, uh, thought of something."

Frannie gave up torturing him and dug into her gingerbread. "The waist thing?"

"Right. That. Now, as I recall, waist measurement is supposed to be a certain percentage of the hip measurement in order to attract a guy."

"What?"

"Yeah, seriously. Sixty percent, I think, but it could have been seventy. Whatever, it was important to a guy who's looking for someone who can successfully support a pregnancy. On a subconscious level, of course.''

"Of course.'' Even on a subconscious level, men made no sense. "So it doesn't matter how thin or fat you are so long as your waist-to-hip proportion falls into the right category?''

Andrew thought about it. "I guess. I mean, it's not like I'm a sociologist or anything.''

No, it wasn't like he was a sociologist or anything. Drew Wiseman was an environmental engineer, and a darn good one at that. Fifteen years ago, when he'd first started coming around, Frannie had been nine and in the third grade. Drew had been fourteen and starting high school a year ahead of schedule. Skinny and small, he'd needed a friend, and her brother had taken the new kid under his wing. In exchange, Drew had seen Rick through four years of math, chemistry and physics. Oh yeah, Drew was bright and he'd been unfailingly tolerant of Rick's little sister. For Frannie, Drew had just been sort of…there, another male in her life trying to tell her what to do, just like her four brothers.

Drew's growth spurt had come late, not until seventeen. Girls matured earlier than boys and Frannie had been a bit advanced anyway. Her hormones had kicked in right around that same time. She'd noticed him all right and had harbored secret hopes for twelve long years. Secret hopes she'd never told another soul, certainly not her brothers, who'd have teased her unmercifully.

Well, a dozen years later, she was seriously considering giving up. Drew seemed hopeless, although she thought there'd been a few positive signs tonight. Still, the bottom line was Frannie wanted a family. Time to go to plan B.

Frannie smiled to herself. Putting plan B into motion had the plus of making Drew squirm as she asked personal questions. It also had the added advantage of letting him know she was soon to be off the market. Maybe, just maybe, it would wake him up to the positive gem that had been right under his nose all these years. Oh yes, she intended to enjoy this.

Chapter Two

The following Saturday night, Andrew settled in to try and watch the Final Four with his buddy Rick. The March Madness Collegiate Basketball Tournament, he'd decided, was a guy thing. Imagine kicking somebody out at half time. So he'd yelled a bit. Heck, he'd learned everything he knew about sports from Frannie's brothers, the prime bit of information being all referees needed glasses. Frannie should be used to it. She was just on edge, Drew surmised. After all, how could you disturb the neighbors when Rick had assured him every household in the country was tuned in? The neighbors were no doubt watching the same game, disparaging the same referees. Frannie, who'd grown up in a house full of males, who could yell and criticize the umps with the best of them, was forgetting her roots. That was all.

"Your sister's gone wacko," he informed Rick as they settled onto Rick's living-room sofa, each with his own steaming bag of microwave popcorn and a beer. Andrew dragged a section of old newspaper over to the beaten-up end table and set his beer on that. Coasters were for girls and the day Evie talked Rick into using them was the day he and Rick stopped being friends.

"I'm serious," he said when Rick merely grunted at his diagnosis of his sister. Drew had sort of bought into this sports as appropriate male entertainment thing, but Rick needed to understand that some things, his sister's mental deterioration, for example, took precedence over basketball.

"Shh, I don't want to miss the tip-off."

"She came by my place last week. Knowing I'd just come back from being out of town, she brought homemade cookies. The woman's devious, I tell you. Devious. She knew I'd be weak. She knew I'd do or say just about anything to get my hands on those cookies. They were fresh out of the oven, Rick. They were still warm. You should have smelled them."

"Hang on just a second." Rick gestured at the screen with a disgusted hand motion. "Aw, man, did you see that? What was that guy, sleeping standing up?"

"Honest to God, all the woman talked about was this bizarre husband hunt she's on. She gave me less than a week to do a bunch of research for her. Otherwise she was going to freeze the rest of the cookies all for herself." Drew was getting incensed all over again just thinking about it.

"Hell," Rick grunted. "You're good at research. You no doubt did a great job, so quit your bellyaching."

Drew slanted a disgusted look at the television. Honest to God, who could care about basketball just then? Another crime he could lay at Frannie's doorstep. She'd ruined the sport for him. "I don't think you're really listening here, Rick. I'm telling you, she's dead serious about this garbage. I've never seen anybody so focused. That general, you know, what's-his-face Schwartzkopf should have been half as focused during Desert Storm. They'd have pulled the entire war off in a day and a half."

Rick jumped to his feet, both hands in his hair. He pulled them straight out leaving his hair standing straight out in spikes on either side of his head. "Charging on Gonzaga? I don't think so! The Wisconsin player wasn't set. He wasn't set, ref. Where's the instant replay? I want to see the instant replay. Do you believe that?"

Andrew's eyes flicked to the TV screen. "Twenty-four was set."

"Hey, remember me? I'm the one taught you everything you know about sports. I'm telling you, he wasn't set."

"Yeah, he was. Sea foam and apricot, Rick. I'm telling you, she's already got the damn colors picked out for the wedding. And what kind of colors are those, anyway? Some guy's going to go into a tux shop and ask for a sea-foam-green cummerbund? Or even worse, 'I'd like an apricot cummerbund and matching handkerchief, please.'" Andrew rolled his eyes at both the play on the screen and the painful mental image. "Like it's not bad enough you have to wear patent leather shoes with a tux. Hell, it's bad enough you have to wear the tux at all. If you have to get married, what's wrong with being comfortable? Jeans and sneakers, something that's not going to literally choke you while you put the proverbial noose around your neck."

Rick watched the TV intently. He didn't sit until the end of the replay. "It might have been charging," he admitted grudgingly. "Maybe." He flicked a glance at Andrew. "Now would you kindly shut up about Frannie and her fictitious wedding plans? I'm trying to watch a game here. It's not like anybody's asking *you* to wear an apricot cummerbund." Rick leapt back to his feet. "He stole the ball! Look at that, would you? He's going all the way. Two points, yes!"

Drew was just pushing himself off the sofa to turn the television off and force Rick to listen to him when the doorbell rang. Rick's eyes didn't even flicker. Drew sighed and went to answer it himself.

He smiled and nodded recognition. "Ladies. What an unexpected treat. Come on in." Somebody had to play host after all. It was obvious Rick wasn't up to the task. "Uh, Evie, was Rick expecting you?" After his last frustrating half hour trying to get Rick's attention, Drew wondered if Evie knew what she was up against. In fact, Drew briefly considered telling Evie her fiancé should come with a label—Rabid Sports Nut.

"Hey, Drew," the vivacious redhead said as she sailed into the entrance hall, Frannie following in her wake. "Is he here?"

Evidently Evie wasn't expected. This should be interesting. "Yeah." Drew jabbed a thumb in the direction of the living room. "In there. Follow the noise."

Evie crinkled her nose and laughed when she heard a whistle blow, the roar of a crowd and the bellowing of her fiancé.

"Put on your glasses, ref."

"The tournament isn't over yet?"

"Ah, no. Not yet. They'll be down to two teams after tonight. Only one more game."

"Hallelujah." And Evie planted herself right in front of the television. "Hi, lover."

Rick leaned to one side, then the other. "Hey, I can't— oh. Evie. How's it going, sweetie?" Rick's eyes shifted from his fiancée to the corner of the screen left unblocked by her body and back to his fiancée. He sighed, picked up the remote and clicked the TV off.

"The wrong guys were winning anyway," he announced philosophically.

Drew's eyes goggled as Rick stood and with a strained smile, gave Evie a kiss and asked, "What's up?" Must be true love, was all he could figure. Scary.

"Frannie and I were out doing wedding stuff. We figured we'd stop by and get your opinion on a few things."

Rick gazed longingly back at the television. "Just a few things?"

Evie held firm. Start as you mean to go on. "Yes. I'd like your input on the color scheme, floral arrangements, the men's tuxedoes, why you have this need to always be on top—just a few little things like that."

Rick was still lovingly stroking the remote control with his thumb. "Uh-huh, uh-huh, sure babe, whatever you want. You know that."

Drew stifled a laugh and whispered to Frannie, "This could get interesting."

Frannie flushed. She grasped Drew's arm and tugged. "Let's you and I go in the kitchen. Give them a little privacy."

"Not on your life," he shot back quietly. "What's wrong with the man being on top, I'd like to know? I kind of like it myself." Then more loudly, "Hey, Evie, about the men's tuxes, basic black, right? I mean, since I've got to wear one—"

Frannie stomped on his foot. "Hush, this is none of your business." She tugged harder, but it reminded her of the last time she'd had to move the refrigerator to clean behind it. Just about impossible. She braced herself and yanked again. Drew barely budged. She was going to need reinforcements, just as she did for the refrigerator. "Come on, Drew."

"Don't sweat it, Drew. Black is fine. For the jacket and pants," Evie said.

The hair on the back of his arm stood up. Planting himself more firmly against Frannie's surprising strength, Drew quickly questioned, "For the jacket and pants? What does that mean? What else is there? I mean, the shirt'll be white.

Dress shirts are always white. And the cummerbund. Black, right?''

"Welll…'' Evie hesitated and Drew panicked.

"I was kind of thinking…''

God save him from women who thought. "What? What were you thinking?''

"Well, you know how men's formal shirts have those rows of ruffles down the fronts?''

Drew was getting a very bad feeling here. "Yeah? Maybe we could just wear plain white shirts. I don't see why that wouldn't work, do you, Rick?'' He turned to his best friend, hoping for salvation but finding only a wicked grin.

"It's only for a few hours, old buddy. Whatever she's got in mind, it'll only hurt for a little while. Promise.''

Frannie huffed, "Honestly, what a couple of babies.''

"I'll make a deal,'' Evie said. "No ruffles on the shirts, just tucks…''

"Tucks?''

"Tucks,'' Evie repeated firmly. "In exchange for which you will, without complaint, wear a cummerbund that matches the bridesmaids' dresses.

"Take it,'' Rick advised. "It's a good deal. Think of it as the fee us guys have to pay to get exclusive rights.'' He gave his fiancée a sick smile. "We're both going to live.''

Then he whispered quietly, "Just agree, will you? The quicker they're satisfied, the quicker we can get back to the game.''

Drew took a deep breath. "Okay, so what's the color scheme?'' He wasn't at all sure he really wanted to know.

"Well, I really, really love pink, you know…''

"*Pink?*'' Drew exploded.

Frannie rolled her eyes.

Evie patted her hair. "But I think it would clash with my hair so Frannie and I have decided on lettuce.''

"Lettuce? That's a color?"

Frannie patted Drew's arm. She'd all but given up on dragging him out of the room. "A very pale green, Drew. Nothing too threatening, just green. Evie and I thought that since her hair was red, we should surround her with its complementary color, green. The wedding pictures are going to be gorgeous." No need to tell him pink had never really been in the running. It had only been thrown in to make the green sound good by comparison.

"Evie's beautiful no matter what she wears," Rick declared loyally.

"Very good, dear," Evie said and kissed him soundly. "That got you two extra brownie points."

Rick hitched up his jeans. "Yeah? How many do I need for another round of me on top?"

"You *were* listening."

"I always listen to you, sweetheart."

It was difficult to feminize a snort, but Evie managed. Frannie was impressed.

"Okay, so lettuce is a girl word for green, right? I can live with green."

"For heaven's sake, Drew, your masculinity will survive." Frannie gave him a hard tug, caught him by surprise and actually moved him. "Now, come on."

"No, Frannie, wait. This is a learning experience. I want to hear more about this point thing."

She pulled again, gained another few inches. "We are not going to stand here and listen in like a couple of voyeurs while they discuss the merits of...whatever. Remember my virgin ears. Now come *on!*"

Frannie finally got Drew into the kitchen. "Here, sit down." She pulled out two chairs from the kitchen table, pushing him into one. "I've done some figuring. Tell me what you think."

Drew rested his head on his hands. "About what?"

"I went out and bought a tape measure."

"Yeah?" Drew was thirsty. He thought about getting up and checking the refrigerator for another beer but it seemed like an awful lot of effort.

"Yes. So I measured. My waist is twenty-four inches. I wasn't too sure exactly where to get the hips, but I figured take the biggest measurement, right?"

He forgot about the beer. "Uh, sure." Twenty-four-inch waist? That was pretty good, he thought. His own was ten inches larger. Man, he wouldn't miss spanning Frannie's waist with his two hands by much. Should he ever get the urge to try, that was.

"And that would be thirty-seven."

"Thirty-seven?" Thirty-seven what? Oh, hips. That's what they'd been talking about. Wow. He could hardly wait to hear the math on that.

"Yeah, so anyway, I divided it out and got sixty-five percent. That's pretty good, don't you think? You said you thought it was between sixty and seventy percent and I got dead center. But the thing is…"

Drew pulled out a pen from the checkbook in his pocket and did some quick calculations on a napkin from the napkin holder. Sixty-four-point-eight-six percent rounded off to sixty-five, all right. "Hmm? What thing?"

"Well, do you know anything about the bust?"

Staring at Frannie blankly, Drew asked, "What?"

"Didn't it say anything in your reading about ideal bust measurements? You know, bust-to-waist or bust-to-hip ratio?"

Man, he was dying here. Sixty-five percent waist-to-hips ratio and she wanted to talk breasts?

"Uh…"

"I'm a thirty-six C. How does that sound?"

It sounded fine to him. Better than fine. How in heck

could he not have noticed a C-cup right under his nose all
this time? "Thirty-six? C?"

Frannie sat up straight, smoothed her hands down the
sides of her chest, an act that pulled her snug knit shirt
even more tautly across her breasts. "I was always under
the impression that most men were interested in a woman's
chest. I mean they certainly stare at it enough. But all
you've said so far was this waist-to-hip thing. So I was just
wondering."

Drew swallowed. Hard. When had Frannie started wearing tight tops? A man would have to be dead—or very
involved in avoiding lettuce wear—what was wrong with
khaki, for God's sake?—not to notice Frannie's chest in
that shirt. "Uh—" he grabbed the first piece of trivia he
could recall and was extremely grateful he could even remember his name, let alone a bit of trivia "—I think I read
somewhere that average is good."

Frannie pouted a bit at that. "Average?" Women spent
an awful lot of time and effort to make an impression and
appear unique. Bummer.

"Extremes of anything are bad. Somebody eight feet tall,
man or woman, is going to have trouble finding a mate just
like somebody who's really, really fat or super anorexic
looking. So, if you put bust size into that context I guess
that would mean that like, flat as a board or—" Drew made
an exaggerated gesture in front of his chest "—you know,
humongo, your breasts precede you by three feet, well that
wouldn't be good. But C, well that's right in there. At least
that's what I would assume."

"B is average. C is better than average but still not over-
board," Frannie decided.

Drew was more than happy to accept her word for it. In
fact, it was so disconcerting to think of little Frannie as
even having breasts, he cast around for another topic.
"Symmetry. I remember that now. Symmetry's important.

The closer you are to being perfectly symmetrical, the better looking you're perceived."

Frannie looked down, a V forming over her brows. "I'm symmetrical. One on each side. It doesn't get much better than that."

Drew got up and went to the refrigerator. He was going to need that beer after all. He couldn't take much more of this. "I'm talking about your face, not your...you know."

"Oh. Well, same goes. One eyebrow, one eye, half a nose, half a mouth on each side. I pass."

"It's the side part in your hair that throws everything off." He came back to the table, raising a hand to wave off her objections. "Just kidding. Just kidding. Here's the thing. We all *think* we're symmetrical but if you ever took a picture of your face, cut it in half then flip-flopped the half that's left so both sides were exactly the same and printed it out, supposedly we wouldn't even recognize ourselves."

"I don't believe you."

Drew shrugged. "Fine. I've got a digital camera. Come over tomorrow. I'll take your picture and we'll try it."

Frannie slapped the table top. "Done. I'm absolutely positive I'm symmetrical."

By the time Frannie and Evie left, Drew and Rick had missed the last of the ball game. It was okay by Drew as they managed to pick up the score on the late-night news—Drew's team was still in there, and he had more important things to discuss with Rick anyway. He picked up beer bottles and carried them from the living room to the kitchen, tossing them into the recycling basket. Rick followed with the empty popcorn bowls.

"I think she's really serious about this, Rick."

"I keep telling you, man, you've got to pick your fights especially when it comes to women. So we wear green cummerbunds for a few hours, even pastel green ones. Next time you want a night out with the guys, you've got leverage. I wore lettuce for you, babe, that's what you say and off you go. They can't say anything because it's the truth. Weddings are important to women. Don't ask me why, they just are. To the guy, it's a means to an end. But women are born planning the big day.'' Rick shrugged. ''Go figure.''

''Rick, could you stay with the program here? I'm not talking about your wedding. That was just a little detour we took because Evie and Frannie showed up at the door. If you don't care that you're going to look like an idiot, then neither do I. I was just taken by surprise is all. I'm talking about your sister. Frannie. Remember her? She's coming over tomorrow so I can take her picture and put it into the computer to check on her facial symmetry. I mean she's *serious.*''

Rick started the hot water after emptying the unpopped kernels into the trash and shaking out the leftover salt from the bowls they'd been forced to use once the girls had shown up. He dropped the bowls into the filling sink and added a healthy squirt of soap. ''Will you quit worrying? Nobody's going to marry Frannie. She's a midget for one thing and for another, she still wears a retainer on her teeth at night so they don't go crooked again. Where's the fun French-kissing a mouth full of plastic?''

''But—''

''Quit your worrying, will you? It's not going to happen.''

Andrew blew out a breath and went to check the living room for any more litter. He found an almost empty bag of chips and another beer bottle that had rolled under the sofa. Man, he felt like Cassandra. At least he thought it was Cassandra. One of those gods or goddesses who was always predicting gloom and doom and having nobody listen.

Rick had everything washed and upside down on the

drainboard by the time Drew got back into the kitchen. He was already swabbing down the countertops although he acted as though there'd been no time lapse in their conversation. "Anyway, if you're all that worried about Frannie, why don't you marry her yourself? I'd trust you with her." Rick shrugged. "I'd feel sorry for you, but I'd trust you. We've been brothers in all but fact for years. Might as well make it real. At least with Frannie you'd know what you were getting."

The beer bottle dropped out of his hand. Drew winced as he heard it break. At least he'd been standing over the recycling bin when he'd dropped it. "What?" he finally gasped. "I didn't hear what I thought I heard, did I?"

Rick threw the sponge into the sink where it landed with a sodden plop. "You heard me, all right. You'd be perfect for each other. You already know each other's flaws. I never understood this aversion you have to marriage. What's the big deal? The drive to create family is a basic instinct, man. Basic. Evie says so. You got something wrong with you is what."

Drew crushed the chip bag in his hand before dropping it in the trash. He only wished it had been Rick's head. "You're the mental one, not me. Anyone with a brain can look around and see that the institution of marriage has severe cracks in its foundation and you'd be a fool to enter the building when it could fall down around your ears at any second. Yet there you go merrily on your way. Well, I'll be the first one to laugh and say I told you so."

"Evie and I are going to be very happy together," Rick got out through gritted teeth. "I happen to believe I'll be the one saying I told you so. Why the hell are you so cynical anyway?"

"Man, open your eyes and look around, would you? Look at my parents. Twenty-eight years, Dad goes into some kind of midlife crisis, has an affair with this woman at work—not even a particularly good-looking woman, which is what really killed Mom—and poof, the whole marriage blows up. Wife number two didn't trust him, with reason since he'd cheated on Mom with her, so that relationship fell apart. He's seriously talking about taking the plunge yet again with some chickee twenty years younger than he is. Think about it. I've got those genes in me. I could do that. Is that what you want for Frannie? Where would she be if I started cheating on her a few years down the road?''

Rick snorted. ''A whole hell of a lot better off than you. Frannie doesn't take crap from anybody, man. She'd take you for everything you had. You'd be the one doing the hurt dance, especially after I got done breaking your face.''

''Oh, and that's supposed to reassure me?'' For lack of anything better to do, he pulled the trash bag out of the cabinet, knotted it off and relined the can.

''Look, all I meant was that Frannie can take care of herself. Hell, you and I are the ones who taught her how. And you should have more faith in yourself. What are you, some victim of your genetic code? You can learn from your father's mistakes, you don't have to repeat them.''

''You're right. Nobody in their right mind would cheat on Frannie. I'm still not marrying her. Remember how close I came with Jayne only to find out she was using me to get through Physics down at Purdue? And then there was Nancy. She didn't want a BA, all she was interested in was an MRS. So long as it was with somebody she thought was going to make enough money to support her in the style she thought she deserved. Permanent relationships are not exactly my forte.''

Rick threw up his hands in exasperation. ''All right, all right. I still think it'd be better for Frannie to marry somebody I know and trust since she's so het up about this. Remember that video we rented from the place that specialized in old movies? *Rosemary's Baby?* Scary stuff. What if she ended up with somebody like that? But I can't hogtie you and force you to the altar. What about this? School will be out for the summer in a few more weeks. Offer her a summer job. She needs one anyway. Let her work in your office. That way you can keep an eye on her.''

The mere idea had Andrew reaching for another beer. It looked like he'd be walking home or camping out on Rick's sofa. He'd had enough to make getting behind the wheel of a car iffy and it was all Frannie's fault. ''No way. You hire her.''

''I'm not the one all upset and worried over nothing like an old mother hen.''

Now his buddy had gone too far. Andrew gritted his teeth. ''I am not acting like a mother hen.'' For crying out loud, how had Rick managed to keep his total lack of intelligence so well hidden? All these years Drew had never even suspected how totally lacking in perception his friend was. Sure the guy had had some trouble in advance placement calculus, but a lot of guys had. Drew had never even suspected.

Drew forced his clenched fists to relax. The temptation to use them on Rick was incredibly strong. One of them had to be mature here, however, and by obvious default, the task was falling to him. ''Listen, Rick, this idea of yours is a good one. You could get her a job at that snooty highbrow law firm of yours. She'd be safe enough there. Bunch of white-collared highly educated mostly married geeks. Can't even understand them when they start in on that legalese mumbo jumbo. What could happen?''

Rick sat down at the kitchen table and ran his hand through his hair. ''Let's see. Where do I begin? Winkley, one of the senior partners, just had divorce papers served on him. Fourth wife. Obviously never played baseball as a kid or he'd have realized three strikes is all you need to be

out. Anyway, word is she's claiming physical abuse. Frannie's tough, but she's also kind of naive, you know? Winkley'd eat her for breakfast. Then I'd have to punch him out.
He's a partner, so I'd lose my job. And it's a law firm, so
he'd also sue my ass.''

"Four? You're kidding."

"Kid you not. And Forter's into women's underwear.
Caught sight of them in the john last week. All satiny with
lace. Frannie doesn't need anybody whose underwear is
prettier than hers.''

"Jeez louise."

Rick nodded wisely. "Yeah. Sick."

"She can't work there. God only knows what else is
going on you haven't uncovered yet."

"No place for a second-grade school teacher," Rick
agreed. "Want me to microwave another batch of popcorn?" he asked, drumming his hands on the table.

Drew waved the offer away. "Nah, I'm okay."

Drew leaned against the counter silently for a moment
thinking hard, then gave up. It was obvious Rick wasn't
going to take his concerns seriously. It was up to Drew to
save Frannie from herself. If Drew hired her for the summer, sure she'd go home covered with dirt at the end of
the day, but at least it was real dirt rather than the meta-
phorical variety. And as far as Drew knew, not a single guy
in his group was into women's underwear.

Chapter Three

"**W**ow. That's amazing."

Actually, it was. "Yeah."

"Who'd have thought?"

Not him, that was for sure.

"So, does this mean neither one of us are likely to ever get married?"

Drew scratched his head as he studied the digital composites in front of him. "Yours isn't as bad as mine," he felt compelled to point out.

Frannie pointed to Drew's picture. "I never realized quite how crooked your nose was. I mean, I always knew it took a bit of a turn, but…"

"Never mind, Frannie, I get the idea," Drew said. So his nose took a slight left hook halfway down his face, she didn't have to rub it in, did she?

"It's just that you assume your face is the same on both sides, you know? But look. I wouldn't even recognize myself as me from this." She pointed to the image where Drew had taken one side of her face and, using its mirror image, made a whole. "Pretty amazing."

Yes it was. Pretty. And amazing. Drew traced the image with his forefinger. And not all that far off. He'd have recognized her from the shot. He took another look at his own composite and grimaced. Talk about unsymmetrical. Maybe he'd be the one who never got married. Maybe the women who'd pursued him had been more impressed by the uniform he'd worn and hadn't gotten around to taking a good look at his face. Who understood women, after all? He should feel relieved. Heck, he did feel relieved. Absolutely he did. Then Drew took another look at Frannie with her hair all loose and curling around her face and the dimple she swore she didn't have peeking out at him.

"Hell," he said.

"Don't take it so seriously," Frannie advised. "I'll just have to work a little harder at this than I thought, that's all. Besides, if you'd just let me take an extra minute to comb my hair the way I wanted to I probably wouldn't look like such a wild woman in the pictures. But no, you're always in such a rush. Anyway, it's my problem, not yours."

Drew turned away to put the digital camera back in its box. He cleared his throat. "So," he began, "speaking of your, uh, problem, have you taken a job for the summer yet?"

"Not yet," Frannie responded thoughtfully but with a small smile. "But I've got some good prospects."

Drew turned back. Hope that he wouldn't have to have her around driving him insane all summer warred with the fear that anything Frannie had come up with was bound to be crazy. Possibly dangerous as well. The woman worked with seven- and eight-year-olds for a living, for crying out loud. What did she know about protecting herself from the wolves and weasels of the world? "Oh yeah? What kind of prospects?"

"Well, for one, you know that billboard you see off on the right side of the road just before you get downtown?"

Drew thought for a minute. "The one advertising the Venetian Festival? Frannie, that's an old advertisement. Venetian Nights are over."

"No," Frannie said, her exasperation evident. "Why would I be interested in that one?"

With Frannie, who knew? Her brain was, to be kind, different, but Drew was just bright enough to keep that tidbit to himself. Come on, now, who picked their future spouse by shopping billboards?

"I'm talking about the one for the dentist."

Drew wracked his brain. "The we're-there-'cuz-we-care-How's-your-bite one?" he asked carefully. It was a totally dippy ad. He sank down into his computer chair, bracing himself.

"Yeah. What about it?"

Frannie leaned forward eagerly in the chair she'd taken. "So I know we haven't done the symmetry test or anything, but he was kind of cute, don't you think?"

Now she thought he went around checking out guys? He didn't think so. He did remember the hygienist on the far left had been kind of fat, but that was about it. "I really couldn't say, but I don't like the way this conversation is headed. You're after the dentist, right? With nothing more to go on than a four-foot-wide billboard smile. Frannie, he could be married. He could be a pervert. He could be into women's underwear, for crying out loud, like this guy Rick knows."

Frannie sat forward in her chair, fascinated. "Rick has a friend who wears ladies' lingerie? Who? Tell me it's Bill McCain. I always thought he was kind of strange."

"Never mind. My lips are sealed."

Frannie laughed and shrugged. She'd get it out of Rick later. "Anyway, I've got an appointment for an interview set up for this week. If he's wearing a wedding ring or has family pictures on his desk, I'll know not to waste my time there and politely turn the job down.''

''And if he's single, you take the job and he turns out to be an idiot, then what?''

She moved her shoulder in a gesture of dismissal. ''Nobody said this was going to be easy. I can't really expect to hit it right on the first try, after all. But if I don't try at all... And, I'll have made more money than teaching summer school. I need a break from the kids anyway. This'll be good for me.''

Aha! Drew jumped on that. ''You want to get away from children? I thought the whole point of this operation was to get you with child.''

''It is. I do want babies of my own. But I want them one at a time. Twenty-five at once can get to be a bit much. Especially when it's raining and they've had indoor recess three days in a row.''

Drew shuddered. It didn't bear thinking about.

''Anyway, I've also been going through the phone book looking at dentists' advertisements. You wouldn't believe how many ads have pictures. I thought I'd call some of the better-looking ones to see about setting up interviews.''

Drew simply stared. My God, the woman was a menace. Rick was wrong, Frannie was a danger to herself and everyone else, but by the time Rick realized it, it would be too late. Frannie could find herself engaged to a silk-panty-wearing weirdo. Women and their stupid biological clocks. Like the world would really suffer if a few of those alarms were left to ring until the battery wore out.

Well, it looked like it was up to him to take charge here. Which was, no doubt, exactly what Rick had hoped for, darn his hide.

He sighed. ''Listen, Frannie, since you're so determined to go through with this, I'll tell you what. I've got some nice guys working for me. Guys who'll play straight with you." God help them. "I always put on some seasonal help. You might want to consider coming with me for the summer instead of the dentist."

Frannie eyed him uncertainly. Something was wrong. This was too easy. She might have to rethink this whole thing. Did she want a guy who was so easily led? "You really want me to work for you this summer?" ·

Drew feigned nonchalance. "It could work for both of us. You could meet some of my engineers. They're good guys." Not that any of them would look too hot blown up larger than life on a billboard, but Frannie didn't need to know that. "And you could genuinely be of help. Looks like I'm going to have a lot of wetlands to put in. Couple of sewage-processing plants and a pig farm for sure want their yucky stuff naturally purified. Maybe a couple of septic fields as well."

Frannie's nose crinkled. "Pigs? Sewage?"

"Hey, I'm an environmental engineer. This is what I do. The stuff's got to go somewhere. You flush the john and it doesn't just magically disappear. Pigs don't just turn into bacon, you know. There's a lot of by-product while they're growing into pork roasts. Didn't you just do Earth Week with your second-graders? Didn't I come in and talk to them about the importance of wetlands in recycling wastes? I'm one of the good guys, lady, and I'm giving you a chance to be on my team for the summer." Digging in muck ought to keep her out of trouble. And eau de swine was particularly hard to get rid of. Wouldn't be too many guys come sniffing around once Frannie started smelling like a sow, now would there? "Come on. Let's go into the kitchen, see what we can dig up. I'm hungry."

Damn shame about her smelling like a pig, though, Drew thought as Frannie breezed by him. She sure smelled good right now. Like chocolate and vanilla with a smidge of some kind of flower mixed in. Lilac or something. Weird combination if you stopped and thought about it. But on Frannie, it worked. Frannie was like that, Drew mused. What would be strange for somebody else was just right for her. Bizarre.

"You got any brownie mix?" she asked. "I could whip some up."

Drew sighed with anticipated pleasure. "Yeah, I've got a box." Frannie made some darn fine brownies. Drew had never quite been able to pull the skill together. The edges were burnt or the center was gooey. Something always went wrong. "I've also got lasagna noodles and ricotta. Maybe you could make a pan of that too?"

She snorted. "Sure, why not? I get to make everything. What's in it for me, buster?"

"I don't have your touch," Drew defended as they entered the kitchen. "And I'm going to make something. I'll make..."

"What? Exactly what will you make?"

"Salad," Drew proclaimed triumphantly. "I'll make some salad."

She didn't look all that impressed.

"And garlic bread." He upped the offer.

"You're also doing the dishes."

He sighed, but nodded acquiescence. It was still a good deal and probably the best he'd get. Frannie was nobody's pushover. No doubt came from being the only girl in a household filled with older brothers.

Thirty minutes later Frannie was layering a main dish of spinach lasagna. A pan of brownies was on top of the refrigerator, cooling, hopefully out of range of a certain twenty-nine-year-old with sticky fingers still unable to delay gratification.

Damn, those brownies smelled good. The smell of hot chocolate literally hung in the air in a rich perfume. Drew inhaled deeply, then moved to get the milk from the refrigerator. He pulled a hotpad from a nearby drawer.

"They're for dessert," Frannie said when she saw what he was doing.

"Some now, some later," Drew said.

"You have to eat the good stuff first," Frannie insisted.

"I'm not one of your second-graders, Frannie," Drew shot back. "I think I can take a little personal responsibility for my own well-being."

Frannie moved to guard the refrigerator. "You hardly touched the salad the other night. Too many oatmeal cookies is my guess."

Drew rolled his eyes. "There were raisins in the cookies," he defended. Damn, but she was a nag. "They count. And oatmeal's good for you. Besides, I'm an adult. If I choose to go without my veggies, it's my choice, now, isn't it." It wasn't a question.

But Frannie was a natural-born caretaker, no matter what feminine liberalism she spouted. "Even so—"

Drew rolled his eyes. "You're never getting married, girl. You're entirely too bossy. No guy is gonna put up with you. Face it. You'll be single forever." And a certain amount of inexplicable relief came with that realization. He enjoyed dropping by and arguing with Frannie. He enjoyed snitching her cookies and brownies when the mood moved him. He liked the way her brown eyes snapped when he got her all irritated—like now. And it was so cute the way the back of her hair got all spiky from running her hands through it after a hard day in the classroom or when one of her brothers—or Drew—bugged her. It was sticking up right now. Simply put, Frannie made him smile.

Though just an inch over five feet, Frannie was also a scrapper. She got in a couple of good swats when Drew simply reached over her, broke off a chunk from the brownie pan and nibbled a dangling edge. Darn, it was hot.

"Ouch. Cut it out." He swore as he swiveled away to protect his ill-gotten gains.

"You are such a jerk."

"I said I'll eat some damn salad, now stop. You're going to make me drop it." Drew was trying to juggle the still-hot brownie chunk while trying to fend off Frannie. It was like trying to swat an annoying yet agile little gnat with one hand behind your back.

Andrew defended his treasure until he got to the table. He sat down and poured a glass of milk. "Look," he said and held the glass aloft. "Calcium."

Frannie made a face but admitted defeat. She left him alone. "I suppose I should be impressed. And I don't want to work for you this summer. I'd actually have to listen to you then, and you're an idiot."

Drew shrugged. "Your loss. Sixteen dollars an hour ain't peanuts."

Frannie was amazed and her face showed it. "Sixteen an hour? Man, I'm in the wrong business."

Drew munched away. "Yeah, well when your fictitious children start showing up you'll like teaching. At least you'll have the same work schedule as they do."

Drew sat back in his chair and studied her. "Frannie?"

"Yeah?"

"That billboard thing, you were just kidding, right? I mean, you wouldn't really pick a husband off a billboard or out of the yellow pages, would you? You know there are a lot of nutcases out there, don't you? And not all of them are wearing signs, kiddo. You gotta be careful." He thought of Rick's description of some of the partners in his law firm and shuddered.

"Yeah, well, you know what they say. You've got to kiss a lot of frogs before you find your prince."

"Frannie, this isn't funny."

Good grief, didn't she just know it. From the way her

family and friends treated her, they all assumed it was more by the grace of God that she'd made it to twenty-four. Frannie herself certainly got no credit for survival skills. "Don't worry about it. If Dr. Billboard turns out to be a polliwog I've got a few more ideas up my sleeve."

Drew snorted. The guy turning out to be a polliwog was not what concerned him. And he did not want to hear any more of her harebrained ideas. Unfortunately, Frannie was on a roll and there seemed to be no stopping her.

"Once school is out, regardless of where my summer job is, I'm going to start eating lunch at the deli just north of downtown."

"Jake's?"

"Yeah. It's right by—"

"Logan's Machine Company international headquarters. Man, Frannie, all their upper-ups eat there."

She smiled smugly. "I know. And when it gets crowded like it does at lunchtime I might be forced to ask some young upwardly mobile executive type with a bare ring finger if I could share his table."

His eyes bugged. Women were a lot more sly than even he'd suspected. And Drew hadn't cut them much slack to start with.

Drew blew on his brownie chunk one final time then popped the entire thing in his mouth. Damn, he'd burnt his mouth. Taking a healthy slug of milk, he got out between gulps of cooling air, "Try this on for size, Frannie."

"What?"

He knew Rick's little sister. She might be twenty-four, but she was not free with her favors. "Well, you're gonna have to kiss this guy, whoever he turns out to be, and that's just for a start. You want children. Any guy I know would insist on the old-fashioned way and they're probably going to want a few trial runs to boot."

"I can kiss," Frannie responded defensively. "And

that's as much of a trial run as they're going to get. There's only one lucky guy who gets to undo all the wrappings."

"You almost gagged when Bobby Thornton kissed you. I remember. You came home and told Rick and me all about it. Rick and I really let him have it."

Frannie slammed the oven door on the lasagna she'd just finished assembling and plunked her hands on her hips and gave him her best evil eye. "And you have the nerve to complain that I don't treat you as a grown-up because I wanted you to eat properly. If that isn't a case of the pot calling the kettle black I don't know what is."

Drew swiped his upper lip with his tongue, removing a thin milk mustache and a couple of brownie crumbs. "What? What'd I say now? What's that supposed to mean?"

"It means the incident you're referring to happened in the third grade. I really would have preferred kissing a frog. Then. I grew up, baby."

"You're still a shrimpster," Drew pointed out in an unkind jibe guaranteed to get a rise.

But Frannie failed to fall into old patterns. She merely smiled superiorly. "As a matter of fact, I went to prom my junior year with Bob Thornton. He'd grown considerably since third grade, needless to say. In fact, he was an all-state swimmer by then with shoulders a mile wide. His teeth had been straightened so they didn't stick out all over his face and his bright orange hair had darkened to this really nice kind of auburn shade. We parked around the corner for a while before he brought me all the way home." Frannie smiled smugly and broke off a chunk of brownie for herself. "Let's just say I didn't gag even once."

Drew was scandalized in spite of himself. "Mary Frances Parker, you're making that up. You've never gone parking with anybody."

She gave him a pitying look. "Right."

"Your brothers would have killed anybody who touched you and then locked you in your room until you were forty."

Frannie shrugged. "What they didn't know couldn't hurt me."

Drew still looked shocked and it finally irritated her. "Come on, Drew, I'm twenty-four, not eight. And why do you think I went away to college? My gosh, there must be at least a gabillion colleges and universities within a forty-five-minute drive of here. Notre Dame, St. Mary's, Andrews, Southeastern, Southwestern, Holy Cross, Indiana University South Bend, etcetera and so forth. I could easily have gotten my diploma and never left home."

Drew wasn't willing to risk trying for another chunk of brownie even if it was from his own damn mix so he guzzled the rest of his milk. The glass clattered when he set it down. His hand shot out and stabilized it before it toppled. "But you were so taken with Michigan's campus and their program." He glared at her. "At least that's what you said."

"They do have a good program. Ann Arbor's a nice place. But what I wanted most of all when I chose a college was out from under my brothers' collective thumb."

Andrew got up and paced the length of the kitchen before pivoting quickly. "If you're trying to tell me you went off the deep end in college, got wild and squirrelly, I won't believe you. You graduated early, carried eighteen to twenty hours a semester and had an extremely high GPA in the bargain. Rick bragged about it regularly."

"Only because his wasn't so hot."

"A 3.9 is still a 3.9"

"3.87."

"Close enough." He glared at her. She was lying. Had to be. He wouldn't, couldn't accept anything else.

Frannie stood with her thumbs hooked through her jeans'

front belt loops. She was enjoying shaking his boat. "And I'm not saying I wasn't selective. I was. Very. But I can kiss, Drew, trust me. I can kiss. And with the right guy I don't think it will be any great hardship producing a family. I certainly plan on enjoying the process." She smiled seductively. "And I'll do my best to make sure the lucky guy does too."

Andrew's face grew red. "So you're going to try and snag some guy with sex?" he asked sniffing disdainfully.

Frannie was twenty-four, but her brothers were still quite capable of descending on her en masse. Drew looked very close to the point where he'd call in the troops for support. She didn't need that. She wanted to push him, but not too far. Frannie was walking a fine line and she knew it. It was time to quiet the waters she'd stirred up. "No. I intend to catch him with my sparkling personality, my scintillating wit, my undeniable intelligence and homemaking skills, to name just a few. I'm just saying that once he's good and caught, he won't suffer."

The whole world was just plain off-kilter. His best buddy Rick's baby sister simply shouldn't be talking like this. Sure she was chronologically old enough and everything, but it was just wrong for her to be here in his kitchen talking about kissing and sexual stuff. Plain wrong. And the only comeback he had—"Says you"—was pretty darn lame.

"Yeah, says me." Frannie contemplated Drew for a moment. God, it was tempting to shake him up just a bit more. She bit her lip.

He'd probably run straight to her brothers.

Still, it might be worth it. Frannie narrowed her eyes while she weighed her alternatives. She cocked her head. Some things were worth taking a chance on. She'd waited a heck of a long time for an opportunity like this. Time to seize the moment...

"Wanna see?"

"What?"

Frannie walked up to him, crowding him. It was almost funny the way he backed up. Almost. "You heard me. Wanna see?"

"Frannie—" Her stockinged toes butted right up to the tips of his sneakers. Drew held up a hand, took another step back.

Frannie came forward, crowding him again. "Come on, tough stuff. I don't bite. Much."

Drew's eyes widened.

Frannie almost laughed out loud at the glazed look in Drew's eyes. Darn, this was fun. She ran her hands lightly up his arms to his shoulders, then looped them around his neck. Standing on her tiptoes brought her up to his chin level, so she tugged a bit, just enough to bring his head down to her.

"Frannie, what are you doing?" Drew asked in a desperate and ridiculous final attempt to save a rapidly degenerating situation. It was pretty obvious what she was doing. He felt like he'd entered some alternate world. Some alien life form had taken over the body of the Frannie he knew. Maybe he should be thinking about contacting Ghostbusters. Or the local church clergy. Somebody. "Frannie?"

"If you have to ask, I must not be doing it very well." She breathed on him and he stumble-stepped. That made her feel powerful and she smiled. Oh, it was good to throw at least one of the superior males in her life off balance for once.

"You're the little sister I never had."

"Wrong." Frannie ran the tip of her tongue over her front teeth in a teasing sweep and kept right on crowding him. "There is no blood shared here, not a single drop, buddy." Her hands found his shoulders and squeezed hard muscle.

She was being deliberately provocative, he was sure of it. Well, almost sure. Drew's eyes about crossed. He told himself it was just that she was so close. How else were you supposed to focus? He was starting to feel a bit desperate. "Now, Frannie..." His voice trailed off. Drew couldn't think of a single thing to say.

"Think of it as a friendly kiss," Frannie urged, really beginning to enjoy herself. Drew was just so darn obviously uncomfortable it was amusing. "You know, a casual, good-to-see-you kind of thing."

Now, how could such a mundane sentiment be delivered in such a sultry, husky contralto that it sent a chill down his spine? Frannie was too close, that was all. She had invaded his personal space and he was ill at ease. Drew had read somewhere that it made people nervous when you invaded their personal space. He was sure there was nothing more to it than that.

But damn, what a sweet invasion.

Rick would whomp on him but good if he knew what Drew was thinking right now. Heck, Drew was thinking of smacking *himself* upside the head. This was *Frannie*. Who'd have thought she'd feel so darn good tucked up against him? Her curves were just so...*curvy*. It was throwing him off balance, that was all. He was momentarily, ever so briefly, a bubble or two off plumb. He'd be fine in just a second or two.

Drew put his hands behind his back and clasped them there. "Can we talk about this? I've never seen you give Rick a friendly—"

But Frannie rubbed her chest against his, delighting in his obvious discomfort. "Of course I don't kiss Rick. That would be like kissing the dog. But I kiss Jerry, Steven and Mike hello and good-bye when they come into town." She looked at him through lowered lashes, walked her fingers up his chest. "You just keep thinking of me as the sister you never had and I'll think of you as Jerry or Mike."

Drew gulped. Thoughts of a little sister had never seemed more far-fetched. Frannie's lips were like, *right there* in front of him all pink and full and damp from that last aggravating tongue sweep. He'd never noticed how often she used that facile little tongue of hers to moisten her lips before. Suddenly he wanted to taste her glistening pink mouth more than anything. Heck, he'd be willing to lose his five bucks and throw the March Madness pool to see this kiss through to its completion, although Drew would've given up his wetlands work and taken an indoor, nine-to-five suit-and-tie job before admitting it.

"All right," he finally muttered, deflated by just how easy it was to cave in to the moment. "A sibling kind of thing."

"Right," Frannie murmured and their breaths mixed. "Just a friendly little peck." Yeah, right. Was he ever in for a surprise. She wondered how long it would take her to make Drew forget to keep his hands behind his back. Five seconds? Ten?

Under a minute, for sure she decided and set out to see just how much under she could make it.

Closing the small gap between them, Frannie first traced Drew's upper lip, then the seam between the two. He had a nice mouth. She'd noticed years ago. What a treat to finally get to take it for a test ride.

Holy macaroni. Frannie better not kiss Jerry or Mike like this. Drew's breath hitched at her boldness. Frannie took the opportunity to slip the tip of her tongue inside his mouth and about blew the top of his head off. "Mmmph!"

"Mmm."

Mmm was right. Damned if Frannie hadn't been practicing with somebody. Drew was already tired of being the passive one, and he called his own tongue up to the front and entered it in the fray. Holy smoke. He'd burned himself cooking over fires that hadn't been anywhere near this hot. Oh yeah, he could toast a marshmallow or two over these flames.

Drew forgot to keep his hands behind his back and out of trouble. It was discouraging how easy he was. No more than a few seconds had gone by. He widened his stance and used his arms to snug her body in close. Then he let his hands roam her back.

Frannie's ploy had backfired. Her intention had been to shake Drew up a bit, to show him what he'd been missing all those years he'd been so darned *oblivious*. As it turned out, though, it was Frannie, who'd thought she'd known what she was missing ever since Drew had grown shoulders, who was wrong. She hadn't been expecting this—not every fuse in her brain short-circuiting. It wasn't until well after they'd both stepped back and taken a deep breath that she realized she didn't know if she'd won her bet with herself or not. Frannie *thought* it had been less than a minute before his arms had come around her, but as she'd been too engrossed in the kiss herself to bother with checking the time, Frannie really didn't know for sure.

Well, damn.

Drew took a deep breath. "Holy cow, Frannie. What the heck were you thinking? You can't go around kissing people like that. Have you even heard of the word *platonic?* Do you have any idea of its meaning? That isn't really how you'd kiss Mike or Jerry. Is it? Man, I've got to talk to those two."

Frannie smiled in pleasure. Oh yeah, she hadn't been the only one rattled by that kiss. Just listen to Drew ramble. "I changed my mind."

That stopped him, made him think. "What? You what?"

"I changed my mind about the kind of kiss I was going to give you."

"Changed your—"

"Mind." Frannie nodded. "I decided to practice. Get my mouth back in shape so when I finally have the lucky guy lined up I don't end up fumbling. The old use-it-or-lose-it, you know?"

"The old—"

Oh this was too good. Drew was incapable of completing a sentence. Surely that was a positive sign.

"Man, Frannie, you've got to give a guy some warning. You can't just lay something like that on me without a little notice. You almost gave me a heart attack." He sounded like a fool even to his own ears but just exactly how was he supposed to think of Frannie as the little sister he'd never had after this?

Chapter Four

When he thought about it logically, really dissected that kiss, if it had gone through the movies' rating system the whole scene would have gotten at most a PG13. Maybe. If the censors had been in a bad mood.

So, that being the case, how was it that three months later, March Madness long since succumbing to April angst, May mania and now June jumpiness, Drew still couldn't get that one fit-for-general-audience kiss out of his mind?

It was pathetic. Just look at him. He sprawled heavily in his living room recliner and tried to figure out where he'd gone wrong. Three months was a long time to fixate on one lousy kiss, for crying out loud. He hadn't been able to view Frannie in quite the same big-brother, fondly-indulgent-of-cute-but-annoying-little-sister way ever since—or for that matter, look Rick in the eye. Fortunately Rick was so besotted he hadn't noticed the lack of directness in Drew's gaze. Drew lifted up a bit to adjust his jeans. Damn. He couldn't even think about Frannie without—food,

Drew thought. He needed food. Protein from a USDA-stamped chunk of red meat would take care of what ailed him. The woman had yet to be born who could hold a candle to an All American greasy—none of that reduced-fat stuff—fried burger with a bag of potato chips made with more grease on the side.

Drew grimaced as he hauled himself out of his chair and went out to the kitchen. He grabbed some ground beef from the fridge and, using more force than necessary, beat it into patty form.

Frannie was going to start work at his company the very next day.

Looking down, he realized he'd been sprinkling salt on his hamburger quite a bit more heavily than he'd intended.

"Damn."

He scraped the excess off. She'd probably set everything he'd worked so hard for right on its ear. Heck, look at him, Drew thought as he dumped white crystals into the trash. *He* was already on *his* ear. "Well, it's just not going to be happening," Drew mumbled as he layered on pepper and garlic powder with a far more careful hand. "On company time she'll be planting cattails and that's all there is to that. She'll just have to get with the program," he further lectured himself as he dropped the patty into a hot skillet. "First thing tomorrow morning I'll bring her into my office and lay down the rules. Make them simple and clear so there's no communication problem. Nothing worse than a failure to communicate. Ask Paul Newman."

Which started him thinking about *Cool Hand Luke.*

Which started him thinking about the car-wash scene in *Cool Hand Luke.*

Which started him thinking about Frannie starring in the car-wash scene in *Cool Hand Luke.*

Drew broke out in a sweat. His jeans needed adjusting. Again.

"God," he said. "No," he told himself, proud of how firm he sounded. "Business during business hours. Funny business will have to wait until after 5:00 p.m." He felt better for all of a minute or two. Then he frowned. "Caught between a rock and a hard place," he grumbled. "What kind of choice is this? Let Frannie take my business down by letting her husband-hunt during business hours or restrict her silliness to after hours when I can't keep an eye on her." He ran an irritated hand through his hair. "Man!"

The beep from the smoke detector got his attention. His dinner was smoking. Swearing under his breath, he flipped his burger and smooshed it down with his spatula, then turned down the flame. Drew looked at the stove clock. It was 6:30. There was a movie he'd been thinking about seeing with an 8:00 p.m. show time. He knew because that's what he'd been doing in the recliner chair, looking through the paper, trying to relax after a long day at work before his mind had drifted to thoughts of—you know who. "I wonder if Frannie's seen it?" he asked no one in particular as he lifted the burger from the pan and deposited it on a plate before dropping his bun facedown into the leftover grease to toast it. What the heck. He sliced up an onion and threw that into the grease to fry as well. Heart attack on a plate. He'd always liked to live dangerously.

He decided to give Frannie a call.

"So, what's this movie about?" Frannie asked as she slid into the front seat of Drew's car.

Drew closed the passenger door and circled the car before answering. He switched on the ignition and turned around to look out the rear window as he began maneuvering out of the spot he'd found in front of Frannie's little rental house. "Action adventure," he grunted as he swung the wheel. "You like those, don't you?"

"It's not one of those where everybody dies in the end, is it?" she questioned suspiciously. "I don't like those."

"Sylvester Stallone. He never dies," Drew assured her. "He might get beat up some, but he never dies."

"Sylvester Stallone? Oh, come on. He's got no upper lip," Frannie complained.

"That's the trouble with you, Frannie," Drew complained as he finally worked his way free of the parking spot. "You're never satisfied. Not only has he got more money than he could spend in two lifetimes, the guy's got legs the size of tree trunks, biceps with a thirty-six-inch circumference and a chest Attila the Hun would kill for, and all you can say is he's got no upper lip?" Drew questioned. "Pick, pick, pick. I've said it before, I'll say it again. You ain't never getting married, woman."

Crossing her arms defensively over her chest and sticking out her lower lip, Frannie pouted. "Well I'm certainly not going to marry a modern-day Attila the Hun. Especially if he's flawed. Who'd want to go to bed with a lipless Attila? Besides, there'd be a fifty-fifty chance any little Attilas we had would be born without upper lips too, and I couldn't stand that."

Drew couldn't stand it either, and he damned himself for caring. Still, he pretended to adjust his rearview mirror and double-checked his reflection. No, his upper lip hadn't magically disappeared since picking up Frannie. It was still there, thank God.

Oh, good grief, why did he care? It wasn't like he was in the market to marry her. Not at all. "Look, forget about Sylvester. He was for me, anyway," he got out through gritted teeth. What had possessed him to call Frannie to go with him to the movies? What, he was now into self abuse? "The movie's also got Sandra Bullock. She's for you."

"Oh, so now you're saying Sandra Bullock's got to end up with a no-lip?"

"Grrr..."

Frannie laughed and reached over to pat Drew's thigh. "Oh, chill. I'm kidding. Boy, are you ever easy to get a rise out of. I promise. If Sylvester Stallone ever asks me to marry him, he's got a deal, okay?"

Drew's muscles tensed at the feel of Frannie's hand on his thigh. Damn, how could something so little and light affect him so profoundly? He sure hoped she wasn't looking down because his body was advertising its reaction to her touch. "You're out of luck," he told her. "Stallone's already married. To a Kennedy, I think."

"That's Arnold, not Sylvester. Arnold's married to Maria Schriver, I think." She patted him once more, before removing her hand.

Drew all but sagged in his seat when Frannie's hand finally lifted from his thigh. He blew out a shallow breath as he pulled into a parking spot in front of the theater. Man, if Rick were to catch a side view of Drew just then, he'd probably punch him out. Gamely, Drew tried to keep his thoughts on track. "Yeah, well, I still say he's married. To somebody."

"Fine. He's married. Never let it be said I'm a home wrecker. I'll leave him alone. Holy mackerel, Drew, what is with you tonight?" Frannie asked, giving him a puzzled look as she opened her car door and got out.

Drew took her arm as they walked to the theater lobby. "It was raining earlier," he justified. "Cars leak oil all over parking lots, you know. Then when it rains it gets slippery. I wouldn't want you to fall."

"Yeah, uh-huh," was all Frannie could think to say, trying to think of a single time since she'd gotten out of grammar school that she'd fallen or even slid in Drew's presence in an oily rain-dampened parking lot.

Then Drew paid for her admission. "I'll get it," he'd said, which really threw her for a loop. Usually they went

Dutch treat. Of course, usually they were in a group of Rick and Drew's friends and she was invited along more as an afterthought.

Was this a date?

Drew held the lobby door for her. Frannie had to concentrate to keep herself from biting her knuckle, something she did when she found herself in a situation where she was unsure. Frannie cleared her throat. "Um, since you took care of the tickets, I'll go get the popcorn."

Drew still had his wallet out and waved her off. "It's under control, I've got it."

He was going to spring for the popcorn as well? It had to be a date. Didn't it?

Drew pointed to a spot out of the main stream of people flooding into the theater. "Wait for me over there where I can see you. If anybody bothers you, just yell."

Frannie had to roll her eyes at that. Yeah, St. Joe, Michigan, hotbed of crime. Someone was bound to bother her here in a crowded theater lobby.

"I'll be right back," Drew assured her.

Frannie had to bite her lip to keep from making a smart-aleck retort. There was the slim possibility that Drew was starting to see her as more than Rick's little sister or worse, the little sister he'd never had. She was hardly an unbiased observer, but still, Drew had seemed protective and yes, even a little bit possessive since he'd picked her up earlier. It would be incredibly stupid on her part to do or say anything to make him balk now that he was finally showing a little promise.

"I'll be right here," Frannie said and obediently walked to the assigned spot. Under the pretense of studying a coming attraction poster hanging on the wall behind her, Frannie turned her back and rolled her eyes. Even with the possibility that she was on her first real date with Drew, it could still turn into a very long night. Frannie wondered if she'd be allowed to go to the restroom by herself.

It took Drew several minutes to work his way to the front of the line but eventually he was back in front of her handing over a cardboard bucket of popcorn and guiding her into the darkened seat area with a proprietary hand on the small of her back.

If this wasn't a date it was the next best thing.

His hand burned a hole through her shirt. She shivered in response.

Drew leaned down and whispered, "Cold?"

No. Cold, she wasn't. "I'm fine," she whispered back as she slid into the seat Drew indicated. He'd found them a place off to one side. The spot's chief advantage seemed to be its lack of any close neighbors. It was difficult to read his face in the dark. Had he found them an isolated pocket on purpose? Darn, Frannie hated being in the dark. In more ways than one.

They watched the movie. By the time Sylvester and Sandra had reconciled their differences and were holding hands watching the bad guys turn into toast, Frannie was more confused than ever. Maybe it wasn't a date. Drew hadn't tried to hold her hand or put his arm around her. Nothing. There'd been a few whispered comments, but they'd all been along the lines of, "What? I missed that. What did he say?" And then there'd been the truly romantic, "This is why I'd rather wait for the video. You can't back it up and watch it again when they're mumbling and you can't catch what they're saying the first time. Why do they mumble in the movies anyway?"

"He has a lip condition, remember. That probably makes it harder to talk."

"Shut up."

Frannie grinned but shut up. They sat through the credits so Drew could see who'd sung the title song. Then Drew rose and turned to help Frannie up. "So, you want to go for a drink or something?"

Okay, so maybe it was a date. The roller coasters at Six Flags over Great America had nothing on her emotions tonight. Oh well, she'd always loved a good roller-coaster ride. "Sure, why not?"

Drew nodded and took her arm again—to keep her from sliding on discarded popcorn containers?—and guided her up the aisle and out into the night.

Frannie's arm felt like silk under Drew's hand. It was ridiculously difficult to let go after he'd tucked her into the passenger seat of his car.

"Where do you want to go?" he asked after hurrying around the car and sliding behind the wheel. He turned the key.

Frannie shrugged. "It doesn't really matter. You decide."

They ended up at a small bar attached to a grill. Young singles milled about, leaned on bar stools, several obviously on the make. The noise level was high as people spoke a bit too loudly in an attempt to be noticed, the lights low. Frannie suspected that might be an attempt to compensate for the too-bright smiles beaming at them from all sides.

For the first time since Rick had initially dragged Drew home with him all those years ago, Frannie was uncomfortable with him. She'd run out of small talk. She knew what time to report for work and that casual clothing was appropriate. She'd need to bring sunblock and a hat with a brim. The firm employed about thirty men and women and had its own nursery to grow the plants they used. Lunch was at 11:30. She'd get paid twice a month. Frannie hunched over the small table swirling the ice in her drink and studying the wave pattern she'd set up while she frantically searched for something else to say.

Drew leaned forward before she'd come up with anything. Nodding towards a couple leaning against the bar, he said, "See those two over there?"

Frannie checked the twosome out. From here, it looked like a successful pickup attempt was in progress. "What about them?"

"You peaked my interest with all your questions about what guys look for and how you were going to spend your summer on the prowl. I did some research, read some literature."

Of course. Trust Drew to approach a problem, not by risking getting messy and jumping in with both feet; experiencing, but by going to the library and taking the studious, sanitary method of "researching" the topic to death.

Frannie brought her diet cola to her mouth, sipped. "So what about them?"

"From what I learned, those two are very interested in each other. I don't know who came on to whom but whoever it was is making progress."

Frannie held her glass in her left hand, cocked her head and studied the couple. "They look pretty happy," she agreed. "Animated." She sipped her drink.

"It's more than that," Drew said and picked up his beer. "Look how they're both leaning back against the bar but are angled towards each other. See? He's leaning on the counter with his elbow. Now watch." Drew raised his glass to his lips, drank.

Within seconds the woman was leaning on the bar with the opposite arm. She picked up her drink with the free hand, sipped. Frannie's eyes narrowed as no more than five seconds later the man picked up *his* drink with his outside hand and lifted it to his lips.

"They're copying each other."

"Yeah, it's called mirroring." Drew waggled his eyebrows. "Highly significant in the dating game from what I can tell. Means they're both interested."

Frannie's brow rose. "Oh, really?"

"Yeah." Drew rested one ankle on the opposite knee, bobbed his foot up and down. "Neat, huh?"

Crossing her legs and letting one foot keep time with the blaring music, Frannie nodded. It was kind of interesting, but didn't Drew ever get bored with being an observer? Didn't he ever want to get up and jump right into the fray instead of sitting back and taking notes?

He leaned forward, gestured to another couple. "Doesn't have to be exact, of course. The mirroring. Look at them."

Frannie looked.

"They're well into the mating ritual, just like those other guys I pointed out."

Frannie leaned forward, closer to Drew. To hear better. "Well into it? What do you mean?"

Drew leaned toward Frannie. So he wouldn't have to shout. "From what I've read, basically we're animals. Same as any other when it comes to this courting stuff. We're at the mercy of our hormones, just like any other species. There's a pattern, stages this kind of ritual goes through that seldom varies all that much. See, now these guys," he gestured once more to the new couple. "They've already gotten past the eye-bobbing bit."

"The what?"

"You know, the seeing-each-other-across-the-room thing. Checking him out, but if he sees you checking him out, glancing away, pretend you hadn't been really looking."

Frannie nodded. "Oh. The flirting, batting-your-eyes stuff."

"That, too. You ever watch one of the nature channels? Ever see one of those specials on mating rituals for one species or another?"

"Yeah, I've seen those." She picked out a peanut from the bowl in the center of the table, cracked it open.

"Some of those birds, man, the preliminaries can go on for hours. You know, bobbing their heads, fluffing up their chest feathers, backing off if one or the other gets too close too fast. Seems like forever, but they'll look, bob, break eye contact, even turn away a time or two before anything interesting happens." Drew grabbed a handful of peanuts.

"So we're no better than a bunch of birds?"

Drew popped a nut into his mouth. "Or lizards...or apes." He gestured towards a male, thirtyish, young-professional type. He was leaning back in his seat, hands locked behind his head, elbows wide while he chatted up another same-category-but-female version.

Frannie's brow furled. "Apes?" she asked, breaking the shell on another nut.

"Yep." He nodded in the direction of the yuppie. "The human version of the male ape throwing his shoulders back to show off his pecs and beating his chest to impress his woman. He's interested, all right. And doing his best to draw her in. Now if that was another guy he was talking to?"

Frannie sighed. She hadn't really agreed to go out for a drink for a sociology lecture. "Yeah? If it was a guy, then what?"

"Well, he'd probably be trying to establish dominance by intimidating the other guy with his chest display. You know, leader of the pack kind of thing."

"She could be his boss," Frannie offered, crossing her legs in the opposite direction.

Drew studied the couple. "Nah," he decided. "He's coming on to her." He took his ankle off his knee and reversed supporting legs, took a drink from his glass. "It's working, too."

Frannie sipped her cola and tried to be objective. "You've got to admit, it's a good chest," she said.

Drew immediately scowled. "Yeah, right, whatever."

He cleared his throat. "How'd we get so off-track?" he asked, straightening in his seat and pushing his shoulders back. "We were talking about those two over there."

Frannie bit her lip to keep from laughing, then had to admit Drew could probably give the other guy a run for his money in the pectoral department. Too bad she'd come out without a tape measure. Maybe she'd just start packing one. According to her brothers, she might as well. She had everything else but the kitchen sink in her purse.

Drew got ready to pontificate again. "Now, as I was saying, couple number two has already passed the look-when-the-other-guy's-not-looking-until-you-finally-make-eye-contact stage. They're already into mirroring, but it's not exact mirroring."

"She's tossing her head, flipping her hair over her shoulders," Frannie said, getting back into the spirit. She ran a finger over her eyebrow, just...making sure.

"Preening," Drew labeled knowledgeably. "And look at him. See how he's got his hand leaning against the bar by his side?"

"Yeah. More male posturing?"

Drew shook his head. "Nah. At least I don't think so. I'm hardly an expert. What I think he's doing there is cutting her away from the herd."

Frannie looked askance. "How's he doing that just by leaning his hand on the bar? That's a little far-fetched, don't you think?"

"Not really. Look how effectively he's isolated her from that guy on the stool next to her. He's telling him she's taken, to move on and find somebody else."

"Just by sticking his arm in there?"

Drew nodded knowledgeably. "Yep."

"Huh. Who'd have thought." Frannie shifted her gaze from the couple in question to Drew. Her mouth was opening to ask another question when she noticed the neat pile

of peanut shells in front her, then the more haphazard stack
by Drew's elbow. She took in the glass clasped in her left
hand, matched by the one Drew clutched in his right. Good
God, their legs were both crossed. Not exactly in the same
way but if the theories Drew had been spouting had any
validity, it was close enough for government work. Their
bodies leaned in towards each other and their feet were
even pointing at each other.

Holy mackerel.

Sitting abruptly back, Frannie's mind raced. Were they
mirroring each other? She released her glass and picked up
another peanut, held her breath and waited. Just when Frannie was about to give up, call her experiment a failure,
Drew set his glass down and reached for the snacks. Cautiously, Frannie uncrossed her legs. Six seconds later Drew
followed suit.

This was unbelievable.

Frannie thought hard. So, like, had she totally missed the
coy-eye thing or were they such an advanced couple they'd
just skipped that stage entirely and gone right to the mirroring stuff? If that was the case and their relationship was
on the fast track, why, they could be married sometime
early next week.

Wow.

Getting a little dreamy, Frannie could already picture the
wedding in her mind's eye. She'd float down the aisle on
her father's arm. Her dress would be something medieval
with long sleeves, the bodice dripping with pearls. With an
evil smile Frannie thought about making Drew wear pink
ruffles on his tuxedo shirt just to pay him back for all the
years of frustration he'd put her through. Or she just might
take the medieval theme to its logical conclusion and put
him in tights. That'd get him, but good. And a codpiece.
Oh, yeah. She laughed to herself before a grim thought
decided to taunt her.

On the one hand, there was the chance they were a terribly advanced couple. But, on the other hand, perhaps they were such a pathetic excuse for a twosome that maybe Frannie couldn't remember the eye thing because it had happened five, ten, even fifteen years ago. Whoa. If that was the case they'd be collecting social security before Drew managed to spit out his vows. Frannie grimaced as her mental image changed. She was old, hobbling down the aisle with the aid of a cane. Her bouquet was wired to her walking aid as she couldn't manage both. Her veil listed to one side of her head as it tried its valiant best to cling to the thinning mop of female-balding pattern white hair which had been carefully combed and sprayed into place to cover as much of her pink scalp as possible. She was bent over, and there was a hump in her back. Osteoporosis ran in the family, after all.

Man, if that turned out to be the real thing, she really was going to make Drew wear both pink ruffles *and* tights once he finally realized he loved her, the dolt.

"What's the matter?" Drew asked. "All of the sudden you look kind of sick."

"Headache," Frannie muttered, touching her hair, fluffing it. Yes, it was still there, thick and curling. *Thank you, Lord,* she prayed silently.

"Probably the smoke," Drew said, throwing some bills on the table.

"The noise too," Frannie said, rubbing her temples in an attempt to banish that last unpleasant image. "Did you notice how loudly everyone is talking?"

Drew stood, then drew Frannie up with a solicitous hand. "It's an attempt to get noticed," he said. "Part of the pick-up scene, according to what I've read. Everyone's trying to draw attention to themselves. Talking loud is all a part of that. Come on. I'll take you home."

"Good idea. We've both got to get up for work in the morning."

"Right."

Frannie went to bed that night still unsure whether she'd been out on a date or not. Drew had driven her home and kissed her goodnight. Unfortunately, it had been a peck on the forehead rather than the soul-searing, mind-blending duel of the lips she'd always envisioned.

Lying flat on her back, hands locked behind her head, Frannie stared up at the bedroom ceiling, contemplating her circumstances.

"Basically, life stinks," she decided.

"I've been in love with that man since I was thirteen years old, so who's the one with the problem here?"

She lay there, eyes wide open, thinking about the last eleven years. Eleven years of her life without a moment of encouragement from the object of her fantasies.

"So am I masochistic, or what?"

Thought she was *so* clever. This latest plan of hers had seemed so brilliant. Frannie had been convinced she was a genius. Get Drew thinking about what caused men to be attracted to a woman and surely, National Merit Scholar that he was, he would follow the seed she'd planted in his brain to fruition.

"Yeah, right."

She turned onto her stomach and punched her pillow.

"Jerk! Idiot!" Unsure whether she meant herself or Drew, Frannie continued to complain to her pillow. "A supposed brainiac like that, who'd have guessed he'd be so stuck in concrete learning? I mean, what's wrong with taking the facts and then extrapolating from them?"

Giving the pillows another good whack, Frannie moaned. "Darn it, he was supposed to start off with the attraction facts and then figure out that initial attraction led to marriage, babies. Love, damn it. But no, not Andrew Wiseman. *He's* got to get stuck on the mechanics of the operation and completely miss the wonder of it all.'' She would have belted the pillow once more, but the mood she was in if it got hit much more, feathers would begin to fly and she'd be out one expensive down pillow.

''God, give me strength,'' Frannie prayed. Instead of hitting the pillow, she contented herself with squeezing the life out of it. ''He was supposed to discover the beauty of love,'' she sighed, kicking her feet in frustration. ''If I'd wanted an anthropological or sociological viewpoint on physical attraction, I'd have gone and taken a bloody course on it. Honest to God, why does the man have to be so darned intellectual about everything? Take a subject and beat it to death, why doesn't he?''

Flipping back onto her back, still squeezing her pillow, she vowed, ''Well, no more. Eleven years of heartbreak is eleven years too long. I am not hitting my head against that particular brick wall one more time. Tomorrow morning I'm starting a new job and turning over a new leaf. Yes, ma'am. There'll be no more mooning over Mr. Wetlands, no sirree, not by me.''

Frannie flung the pillow away from her. It balanced briefly on the edge of the bed, then toppled over the edge. Frannie saluted it as it fell. ''Adieu to you, Mr. Wiseman. I don't care what your studies show, I'm done looking for Mr. Good Looking. Providing you ever figured out I was stuck on you, which is a big assumption, let me just point out, why you'd probably say something like it was a leftover from caveman days or something. Yeah, women picked their husbands for their size and strength so their man would be able to care for them and their children. Well, we've come a long way, baby. From now on I'm going to ignore any billion-year-old, hormonal leftovers, yes I am. No more broad shoulders for me. No, not even Mr. Average Shoulders.''

As her new plan began to form in her mind Frannie sat up. By golly, this was brilliant if she did say so herself. ''Handsome men are shallow, everybody knows that. Good-looking guys like Drew, why they can have anybody. Yes, and if you're used to having whatever you want, you don't appreciate it, do you?'' Frannie answered her own question. ''No, you don't. I'm going to find me somebody homely. Somebody narrow-shouldered who doesn't have babes throwing themselves at him. Somebody who'll appreciate their good fortune when they get me.''

Frannie reached over the edge of the bed, grabbed the pillow, lay back down and stuffed it under her head. She turned on her side. ''All this time I've been on the wrong path, but I've found my way now. I have seen the light, praise be and hallelujah. I'm gonna find me an ugly guy who'll know how to love me.''

Frannie closed her eyes, determined to sleep the sleep of the righteous, but even with Frannie's tremendous power of will, it was a bit of a problem.

Chapter Five

Five o'clock in the morning was an ungodly hour of the day that ought to be banned. The alarm had been silenced minutes before, but Frannie was still gathering her strength to haul her sorry carcass upright and face the day. "It's not like I didn't sleep well," she muttered, refusing to admit even to herself she'd lost even a second of rest stewing over Drew. "I couldn't have woken up as many times as I did if I hadn't been asleep, now could I? There just wasn't enough of it. *He* kept me out too late."

Well *he* wouldn't get that opportunity again any time in the near future. Frannie rolled to her side, then off the edge of the bed. She fumbled her way into the bathroom where she left it up to the cool water of the shower cascading over her head to wake her up.

"Oh, brrr," she complained, bracing her hands on the tiled walls. "I'm never doing this again. Tonight it's gonna be lights out by nine o'clock, maybe even eight-thirty." Shutting off the flow of water, she opened the shower door and reached out for a towel. "How am I supposed to attract even a homely guy if I look like something the cat dragged in? We're going for grateful here, not scaring them into taking off for the next county.''

It took a full hour, but by the time Frannie walked out the door at twenty after six she looked a far cry better than the mere human she'd have settled for at five o'clock. Intent on securing the place, Frannie stuck her key in the front-door lock.

Struggling a bit with the bolt, she admitted to herself that she was pleased with the look she'd caught in the full-length hall mirror. ''I could get into casual,'' she'd decided as she'd stared at her image. The loose blue-jean coveralls she'd put on over a snug white tank top, while not elegant were cute. Frannie had turned, checking over her shoulder on the rear view. Yep, even her rear was looking cute to-day. Why hadn't she gotten into overalls before this? Ah, well, better late than never. And she liked the tan work-man's boots she'd purchased and now wore with comfort-able, thick, cushioning socks. The ensemble was topped with a jaunty Chicago Cubs' baseball cap. Frannie tugged its brim again as she locked her door for the day.

She liked the significance of the cap. It would serve as a reminder of her mission. The Cubs were a losing baseball team. It had been years since they'd won the pennant and Frannie wasn't sure, but she didn't think they'd ever won the World Series. And yet, Chicago loved them. Their park was always full and ''Wrigleyville'' was one of the hottest neighborhoods in the city to own property.

Frannie pocketed her keys, tested the knob. ''That's what I'm going to do,'' she announced, turning, ''Find me a lovable loser, make his day.'' She snorted in an unladylike fashion. ''Heck, make his week, his year, his *life*.'' Finally she'd be the one with the upper hand. Giving her cap one last pat, Frannie finished her pivot and started down her front porch steps—and right into Drew.

"Drew!" she exclaimed, coming to an abrupt halt. "What are you doing here?"

He gave her a quizzical glance. "Giving you a ride on your first day?"

"Oh! Well, how, um, nice," Frannie said, nonplused. She was trying to forget him. Why did Drew have to pick today to be considerate? And darn, he looked good. His jeans formed to his thighs just as though he'd put them on wet and let them dry to him. A cream-colored polo shirt with Wiseman Environmental embroidered in navy over the pocket strained to contain his shoulders. The two buttons on the placket were undone, a bit of chest hair glinted there in the early-morning light.

He gave her a puzzled glance. "Isn't it just?"

Smiling brightly, hoping like crazy Drew hadn't heard her mutterings, Frannie adjusted the shoulder strap of her purse and said, "Well. I guess we'd better get going then. Wouldn't want to be late."

"Boss might dock your pay."

"The boss better not since he's the one holding me up."

"Get in the truck."

"Right."

They rode silently for a while, Drew steering his way effortlessly through the early-morning traffic.

"Beautiful day," said Frannie. Never before had she had to search for a conversation topic with Drew and she didn't like it. And just why was she so ill at ease anyway? She was no longer interested in him. She'd crossed him off her list. So what was this tension that virtually hummed in the air around them?

Not sexual tension, that was for sure.

She shot him a sideways glance. Well, didn't he look all calm and unperturbed?

Irritated, Frannie drummed her fingers on her thigh. This just proved her point. She nodded her head in affirmation.

Yes, she'd made the right decision. Just look at him, she thought resentfully, sitting there without a care in the world, oblivious to her turmoil.

Why wasn't *he* searching for a conversational gambit? How come he was so at ease with this interminable silence that stretched between them? Darn it, she'd checked herself out, front and back, in the mirror before she'd left. She'd gone through an hour of effort and knew she looked good. She was cute, darn it. So how come *he* wasn't shooting *her* sideways glances?

Oh, for sure she didn't want him anymore, the dense Neanderthal. In fact, she disliked him intensely, yes, she did. Frannie folded her hands together in her lap. She vowed not to say another word to the man. She turned and studied the passing landscaping out her side window, her lips sealed shut.

"No need to be nervous, Frannie," Drew said as he pulled into his company's parking lot.

"What?"

"I said there's no need to be nervous. Yes, I expect an honest days' work for an honest days' wage, same as anybody else, but I'm not an ogre."

That was a matter of opinion. "What makes you think I'm nervous?"

Drew snorted. "You're sitting there stiff as a board. Look at your hands." He gestured to her clenched fists. "You've got them squeezed together so tightly your knuckles are white. It doesn't take an Einstein to figure it out."

Frannie rolled her eyes. Oh brother, he shouldn't even go there. He was right in one respect, though. He was no Einstein. "I'm fine," she said, grabbing her purse and opening the door on her side.

"Yeah, right." Drew got out on his side and circled around the front of the truck. "It's me, Frannie, your old buddy Drew. I know you."

As if he'd even had a clue since the day she'd turned thirteen and had stopped thinking boys were inherently gross. *Hello? Hello? It's the clue phone, Drew and it's for you.*

Drew grabbed her hand and pulled her back away from the front door to Wiseman Environmental, Inc. Propping her up against the brick facade wall, he leaned into her. "Come on, now, lighten up. We're not going in until you've relaxed."

In about two seconds flat, she was going to knock Drew on his delectable can. Maybe she wouldn't lust after it so much once she'd put a few dents into it. Closing her eyes, Frannie prayed for strength. "Drew, let it go, will you? I'm fine. Absolutely fine. Rick's wedding is next weekend and I'm a little preoccupied, that's all."

Drew rolled his eyes. "Don't remind me. I'll probably trip going down the aisle on that damn runner you women are insisting on." He studied her face intently for a few more moments. "All right, if you're sure that's all it is."

"I'm sure," Frannie insisted stubbornly. "Now open the door, will you? I haven't been inside your place since you remodeled."

"Let's do it then," Drew said. He opened the front door to his company and ushered her in.

"Wow," Frannie said, suitably impressed by what she saw. "Nice."

Drew looked around, squinting as he tried to see it through her eyes. The walls were cream, the carpet a deep loden green. Large-size professionally framed Before and After pictures of some of his company's work hung on the walls along with botanical drawings of wetland plants and grasses. The receptionist's counter was oak with a natural stone top on it. It *was* nice, if he did say so himself. Professional.

"Thanks," he said, not willing to admit how often he'd

second-guessed the decorator he'd hired to do the job, arguing with her over every choice she made. The office had turned out nicely in spite of his interference.

"Hey, Drew."

"Hey, yourself," Drew responded to the casually dressed bearded man coming around the corner. "What are you doing here so early?"

"I had some drawings to get done for the Stamford project. Who's this?" the Paul Bunyan lookalike asked, his eyes falling on Frannie.

"Rick's little sister," Drew said dismissively, his mind already on the Stamford problem. "Remember, I told you I was hiring her for the summer?"

"You said she was in school."

"I said she taught school. Clean out your ears, man."

"I thought she was seventeen or eighteen, you know in high school or college."

"No, she's, uh—Frannie, how old are you, anyway?"

Rolling her eyes, Frannie filled in the blank. "Twenty-four."

That stopped him in his tracks. His eyes swung from the papers he'd picked up to Frannie. "No way."

"Way."

"Wow," said Paul. "Nice."

"Thank you," Frannie responded with a smile. Drew was still staring at her, eyes narrowed. He looked like he was all set to begin counting on his fingers. "Drew, you and Rick are five years older than I am. Remember? You were starting high school and I was going into fourth grade when you moved here? You're twenty-nine, I'm twenty-four."

"That's impossible."

"Are you or are you not twenty-nine?"

Drew nodded. There was no denying it. He was twenty-nine.

"Then I'm twenty-four. Which works out quite nicely since I graduated from college three years ago and have been teaching second grade ever since."

"It certainly works for me," said Paul, rocking heel to toe in his size-twelve boots while he surveyed Frannie from top to bottom with an unholy grin showing through his facial fur.

So Drew was allowed to mature while Frannie was to remain a child. Fine. She was no longer interested in him anyway. With a sniff, Frannie turned her attention to Paul. Sticking out her hand, she introduced herself. "Hi, I'm Frannie. What kind of drawings are you going to do?"

He wasn't as large as the original Paul Bunyan, but he was no shrimp, either. So while his hand didn't totally engulf hers, it didn't miss doing so by much. Frannie smiled at him as they shook hands and gave him a quick once-over. No point in wasting time. He wore low-riding, much-washed, faded jeans with a thick, well-loved leather belt. A blue denim shirt with Wiseman Environmental neatly embroidered over the pocket was buttoned and tucked into the jeans. A navy T-shirt peeked through the open V at the neck. Construction boots protected his feet.

He let go of her hand after a firm shake. "Paul," he said by way of introduction.

Frannie's eyes widened. "You're kidding."

"Kid you not. Why? Were you traumatized by somebody named Paul in a former life?"

Frannie shook her head and waved away her comment. "No, no. You just, um, look like a Paul to me so I was surprised that it was really your name."

Paul hooked his thumbs into his belt loops. "Cross my heart and hope to die. Paul Campbell. And I'm twenty-six," he supplied helpfully.

Blue eyes twinkled at her and Frannie wished there wasn't so much reddish-brown scrub hiding his face. The eyes were good, a pale sky blue rimmed with navy surrounded by thick dark lashes. If the rest of his face was equally up to snuff he might be too good looking to be in the running here.

Perhaps he'd grown the beard to camouflage a weak chin?

One front tooth ever so slightly overlapped the other when he smiled. Frannie took that as a good sign. Yes, probably he had a receding chin. Or maybe there was no chin problem but he'd had scarring acne. That would serve just as well she decided. In fact, she'd prefer it. There was a lot a good dermatologist could do to keep acne under control these days whereas a weak chin could be passed down. There wasn't all that much you could do about that without breaking the poor kid's face and resetting all the bones. No thank you.

Meanwhile, she'd be nice. Just in case it turned out that he qualified as her Prince-not-so-Charming. "It's a pleasure to meet you, Paul." She nodded at the pad of drawing paper he held under one arm. "What are you going to draw? I can make a pretty mean turkey by making a contour drawing of my hand. The thumb becomes his head and the four fingers are the tail feathers. My second-graders loved it. Maybe I could help you. Need any turkeys in your drawing?" She grinned.

Paul laughed, clearly delighted with her silliness.

Drew rolled his eyes, disgusted. He'd never realized what a sap Paul was. At least when it came to women. It just went to show you, you needed to look at more than a GPA when you hired a guy. Well from now one he'd take their sap factor into consideration as well as their grade point average.

Drew searched his mind. Just who was Paul dealing with over at Stamford? He'd better find out if it was a man or a woman and go over the contract with a fine-tooth comb before he signed it if it was the latter. Geez oh peez, look at the two of them making goo-goo eyes at each other when they'd barely even met. Drew could hardly refrain from groaning out loud.

He'd forgotten about Paul breaking up with his long-term girlfriend last month. With only one-seater private bathrooms in the building, it would be difficult to check out Paul's choice in underwear, Drew realized. Well, he'd just have to keep a closer eye on Frannie, that was all. Thank God the rest of the guys wouldn't be a problem. Paul was the tallest of the lot as well as the best-looking. As cute as Frannie was, she wouldn't be interested in any of the rest. Why should she? She could have her pick, after all. In fact, Drew was rather surprised at the way she was flirting with Paul. Sure, he was decent looking. Paul wouldn't start any babies crying or set dogs howling or anything. But he was no Greek god, either.

Frannie should be more discerning. You shouldn't just come on to any old body, for crying out loud, no matter how desperate you were for a baby. You were talking shared genetic material here, after all. Any kid of Frannie's was already going to be half crazy as it was. There needed to be a weeding-out process, focusing only on likely candidates with good, strong and in this case, dominant genes. Otherwise you'd be spinning your wheels, never get anywhere. Plus, he didn't want her breaking Paul's heart. He'd never get any work out of the guy if she did that. Yes, he was going to have to talk to Frannie.

Scowling, he took her arm. "I think Paul can handle this one all on his own. It's a sewage recycling plant. No turkeys involved unless you count the human variety. Now come on. I've got some filing you can do while we wait for the rest of the guys to come in."

Frannie looked down at her brand new pre-faded coveralls. "Filing? I got all dressed up like this so I could file?

Drew, I want to be outside." Spending time with the guys, not stuck in the office with you when you're officially out of the running.

"Don't worry, don't worry, you'll get there. You're going to be my jack of all trades, official go-for. You knew that. Filing now, outside stuff in a little bit." For crying out loud, it was going to be tougher than he thought keeping tabs on Frannie this summer. Maybe she'd have been better off at Rick's firm this summer looking up precedents in the law library.

Drew thought about the panty-wearing senior partner. Not.

He was brave, he was strong, he could handle this.

"Drew, how organized do you want this? Should I just throw all the B's in together or do you want them sub-alphabetized? It's so great working with real file cabinets. Our school district can't afford them for the classrooms, only the office. I've got nothing but a beat-up old hanging-file container and that was this year. Before that it was cardboard-box city."

Oh, God. Drew's head sank into his hand. It was going to be a long summer. He just hoped his business survived.

"Uh, Frannie? I really need them sub-alphabetized, okay?"

"Sure thing, boss." Quietly humming the ABC song, Frannie set to work.

Picking up the Stamford contract, Drew tried to concentrate. It was going to be a *very* long summer.

Forty-five minutes later, he gave up. Frannie had put on some kind of light but definitely detectable perfume or something. Either that or the soap she used was potent stuff. Drew guessed he'd have to talk to her about that as well. You didn't want to be wearing any kind of scent that would attract bees when you worked outside. And right about then Drew's sympathy lay totally with the bees. How could you fight this kind of thing? That darn perfume Frannie wore was so compelling he was actually gripping the edge of his desk to keep himself from scooting his chair over by the file cabinets with an offer to help. His mind was so addled, Drew found himself actually humming along. "Q, R, S, T, U, V, W, X, Y and Z." He couldn't take it any more. His expensive interior-decorator-designed office had grown positively claustrophobic. He had to get out of there.

"Let's go check on the plantings we're going to use on this next job. They're out in the nursery." Maybe the fresh air would dilute her perfume to the point where he could function, at least minimally. Was she really twenty-four? Drew shook his head. The evidence was irrefutable. Frannie was right. He was twenty-nine. Five years difference made Frannie twenty-four. Nobody would exactly be robbing the cradle if they took an interest, now would they? Drew dragged in fresh air as he slapped the building's back door open and stepped out.

"Wow," Frannie said as she took in the greenhouses and fields behind the main building. "This is really impressive, Drew."

He drew his shoulders back, his chest expanding like a rooster set to crow as he surveyed his domain. "Thank you."

"You're welcome." It really was something. They were now standing in some kind of garden thing. The area was probably used to show customers what type of finished product they could expect. A picnic table sat close to the back door, obviously meant as a peaceful spot for employees to enjoy their break or lunch outside. Outside the small patio area a bark path wound through waist-high ornamental grasses of various descriptions. Water bubbled in an almost-hidden artificial pond, bringing into play the sounds of nature as well as the sights. Plants were labeled with discreet small signs with their name and usage. Beyond that were six metal frame structures that looked as though they'd been shrink wrapped in plastic—the greenhouses. And just past that was a verdant open field plowed with neat, straight lines. Young something-or-others were already growing, a good eight inches high and reaching strongly for a blue sky unmarred by even the hint of a cloud.

It made for quite a view.

"You must be very proud of this, Drew," Frannie said sincerely.

Drew had become so involved with the day-to-day running of things, he suddenly realized how long it had been since he'd taken the time to stop and appreciate how well things had come together for him. Frannie's comment brought him a little moment of epiphany, made him stop and think. "I am."

"How come you never showed all of this to me before?"

There was no ready answer for that. "I don't know," he said, and he didn't. "I guess I didn't realize you'd care."

Well that hurt, but made sense. She was perpetually twelve or thirteen in his eyes, after all. "Has Rick seen it?" She waved her arm in front of her. "I mean all this, not just what you can see from the street."

"Sure he has." Drew wracked his brain. At any rate, he knew they'd run by the office for him to pick up paperwork now and again, just like they'd occasionally cruised past Rick's building. "At least I'm pretty sure he has."

"You should be proud of what you've accomplished here, Drew. Rick's your best friend. He should have been all through this, seen the whole thing."

Drew scratched his head. "Frannie, Rick's a fancy lawyer, spends his time running around in five-hundred-dollar suits. What does he care about my cattails and bulrushes?"

"If he doesn't care, then he doesn't deserve to be your friend," Frannie insisted stubbornly.

"Okay, okay, I'll drag him over some time soon, all right? Sheesh!" Drew strode down the bark path towards the greenhouses with every evidence of impatience but also feeling just a little bit taller than before. He'd impressed Frannie. Cool.

"Hey, Miguel, you seen Brian?"

"I think he's in number five, Drew, culling the stuff for today's plant."

Drew nodded his thanks, waved his hand and was off, heading for the second greenhouse from the end. Frannie scurried after him. Man, the guy had long legs that could really eat up the ground. She'd thought it was hard to keep up with second-graders who never walked when they could run. Drew had missed his calling. He should have been a teacher. He'd have no difficulty whatsoever riding herd on a bunch of eight-year-olds.

Catching the door to the greenhouse before it caught her, Frannie almost plowed into Drew's back. "Oops. Sorry, Drew."

Drew pivoted, steadied her, then slung an arm around her shoulder. "Take a deep breath, Frannie. Breathe. Isn't it great? You can literally smell life growing in here, can't you?"

Frannie inhaled deeply. She smelled peat moss, damp earth and the musty odor of compost. Life growing? She'd never really thought about it before, but could be. One look at Drew's face told her it would be pointless to deny at least the possibility.

"And just listen. Hear that?"

What? Frannie strained to hear. Ever so faintly, leaves rustled gently as the warm air inside the greenhouse was stirred by a couple of large overhead fans. Water trickled in the aftermath of an automatic irrigation misting system shutting down.

"You know," Drew continued before Frannie had half

a chance to respond, "I can remember my parents dragging me to church one time as a teenager and at that age, trust me, they had to drag me."

Frannie laughed. She remembered a few scenes at home between her parents and Rick as well.

"Anyway, this one Sunday the talk was about how some guy had come in complaining that it was really unfair that in the old days God spoke directly to the prophets, told them up front what he expected, but not us. No, he leaves us hanging, wondering what to do, what He wants from us."

Frannie had never really thought about it before. "Some kind of direct communication link probably would be easier," she decided then and there. "But if they had trouble laying the transatlantic telephone cable, I don't even want to think about trying to hook up heaven and earth. What did the minister have to say?"

"He said God does still speak to us. He said that nature was His voice."

Frannie's brow rose. Wow. Heavy. And it had come from Drew. The man had unplumbed depths, that was for sure.

Drew cocked his head. "Hear that water dripping?"

"Yeah?"

"Logically I know it's coming from a man-made hose that's probably leaking and needs to be fixed, but can't you just hear Him? All these years later I still remember that sermon and you know what? It really affected me, even changed my career choice." Drew shrugged. "Like every other little boy I was going to be a race car driver. Or a cowboy, either one. Then I went through my soldier phase. Everyone knows girls are suckers for a uniform, and I needed help paying tuition so ROTC was the answer for a while. I was a slow learner, but finally I got it straight.

"I'm not much on organized religion, Frannie, but every

time I reclaim a wetland area we've managed to destroy or put one in to help process waste material, I feel like I'm giving Him a helping hand. Stupid, huh?''

Well, darn. Just how was she supposed to write off as hopeless a man who saw his work as one giant sacramental moment? Hmm? Just how was she supposed to do that? She stared at Drew. There were areas where the guy could be amazingly shallow and wouldn't it be polite of him to at least be consistently shallow? But oh, no, not Andrew Wiseman, God forbid *he* should be cooperative in any way, shape or form.

It was all Frannie could do to refrain from giving Drew a good quick kick in the shins for being such a lovable jerk.

And then, with the literal blink of his eyes, the moment was gone. Drew's eyes, the windows to the soul, so Frannie had heard, pulled their proverbial shades down and Drew was back to being Drew again.

''Sorry about that,'' he apologized, quite unnecessarily in Frannie's opinion, but that was a guy for you. ''I don't often get all philosophical like that.'' Drew rubbed his hands together. ''Well, let's get ready to get dirty. This is the best part. Getting out here and making stuff grow.''

''I could have guessed that,'' Frannie said as Drew, forgetting to remove the arm he'd dropped over her shoulders, guided her down the main greenhouse aisle.

His mind already busy, wondering if there were enough Juncas for all the upcoming jobs or if they'd need to start more peat pots, Drew responded distractedly, ''How so?''

Frannie rolled her eyes. Could he really not know how easy he was to read sometimes? At least about his work the man was an open book. ''Drew, you couldn't sit still when we were in your office. If fire ants had gotten this far north yet, I'd have suggested retreating to the bathroom and shaking out your pants.''

Drew remembered how the faint whiff of Frannie's perfume in the confined space of his office had rattled him. He flushed. "I wasn't that bad," he muttered.

"Oh yes, you were," Frannie assured him. "As soon as we stepped outside it was obvious this was your true element."

Drew barely refrained from snorting. He wasn't going to be the one to explain that out here the light breeze had blown away her scent. He could breathe again. He was safe as long as he stayed upwind of her. Of course, wasn't it just like a woman to remind a guy of things they were better off forgetting? Suddenly he couldn't fill his lungs again without getting a snootful of essence de Frannie. *Thanks a lot, Frannie.*

"Whatever," he said. "Hey, Bri," he called. "You in here?"

"That you, Drew?" came a disembodied voice.

"Yo. Where are you, man?"

A head popped up one row over and about fifty feet down. "Over here. We got a leak, big guy. I'm trying to figure out what's going on. Hey, who's this?" The head rose, developed a body and all of the above came to attention, focusing on Frannie much like a setter sighting a plump little pheasant.

Drew steered Frannie up the row and over one. "Brian, this is Frannie, my buddy Rick's little sister. You think we should start some more cattail, Bri?"

"What? Cattail? No, man, I think we're pretty well covered. I thought the kid you were bringing in was some highschooler."

Frannie sighed, shook her head. Was that how Drew subconsciously thought of her? Was that why everybody who worked in this place seemed to think she was about ten years younger than she actually was? She stepped forward, hand extended. "Hello, Brian. Nice to meet you."

Brian wiped his hands on his pants, checked them visually, then held them up defensively. "Sorry, but I don't think you want me to touch you. It's still a pleasure meeting you, though."

"Thank you."

"Brian," Drew prodded. "The cattails?"

"Hey, I can count them up if you want but, like I said, I think we've got it covered. You, uh, want me to show Frannie here around?" Brian asked, sounding hopeful.

"I think I can handle the tour," Drew said dryly.

Frannie smiled as sweetly as possible through gritted teeth. How was she supposed to make time with any eligibles if Drew kept her glued to his side? "Thank you for offering, Brian. I'm sure I'll be coming to you with a million questions and be driving you mad in no time at all."

"Impossible," Brian insisted. "You come to me anytime. Ask me anything."

Frannie dimpled. "I'll do that. Thank you."

Drew gave Brian an odd look, pivoted, then said to Frannie, "Come on. I want to check the other greenhouses," before giving Brian one more puzzled look over his shoulder.

"Are all these cattails?" she asked, gesturing to the hundreds of little plants huddled together in long rows.

"Scirpus, Typha and Juncas," Brian eagerly called to her retreating back before translating, "Bulrushes, cattails and reeds."

"Why so many?" Frannie asked, trying to turn again and talk to Brian, though Drew wouldn't let her.

"It requires a heck of a lot of oxygen to bring the BOD in wastewater under control. The Natural Resources Conservation Service has done a lot of studies—"

"The what? The who?"

Drew sighed. It was going to be a long summer. Not only was her perfume going to make him bonkers, Frannie was clueless when it came to the job he wanted her to do. He should have hired a biology major. Botany. Earth science person. Anybody but a second-grade teacher playing husband hunt.

"Gotta go, Bri. See you," Drew called, dragging Frannie behind him. "Don't worry, I'll fill her in so she doesn't make you nuts." Holy smoke. Brian was a great guy, but not exactly Mr. Good Looking. Drew didn't even want to think about a symmetry study of Brian's face. He had the next best thing to a unibrow, his nose took a left followed by a sharp right and at twenty-seven, he'd finally had braces applied to teeth that were a jumbled train wreck inside his mouth. What the heck was Frannie thinking of, smiling like that at him? Why, she was going to break the poor guy's heart when he realized she didn't mean anything by it. He really, really was going to have to talk to her. Maybe she hadn't dated enough to understand. That was probably it. Frannie would just have to curtail all that natural friendliness and interest she displayed to everybody and everything before every guy in the place claimed she'd led him on. The entire firm would be in an uproar. Chaos would reign. The sun would refuse to shine. Night would overtake day.

It was all up to him.

Chapter Six

"What is the matter with you?" Drew hissed as he led Frannie away.

Frannie looked at him askance. "Me? What's wrong with me? I was just going to ask you the same thing. Would you please stop pulling me along like a caveman dragging home the spoils of war?"

"Maybe when you quit acting like one. For God's sake, Frannie, you can't go up to every guy you meet acting like a lost puppy looking for a home. Somebody's going to take you seriously."

"What?" Frannie dug in her heels. She was still moving forward, but at least she'd slowed him down some. "Excuse me?" With her free hand, she grabbed on to a support pipe, almost pulling her arm out of its socket as they ground to a halt. "And just what is that supposed to mean?"

Drew gave her a tug, got nowhere. "Let go, will you? Before you pull the entire greenhouse down on top of us. Wouldn't that just be the capper." It wasn't a question.

"First you tell me what you meant," Frannie said, hanging on for dear life and praying like crazy Drew would give in before she dislocated something. But really, she couldn't let him spend the summer dragging her from pillar to post, now could she?

Drew dragged off his Pacers' cap then jammed it back on in frustration. "For crying out loud, Frannie, you're not dealing with a bunch of second-graders anymore."

"I never thought I was," Frannie shot back, insulted by the accusation. Anyway, last time she'd made a construction-paper birthday hat for one of her teacher friends, treating her like a child, the woman had loved it.

"You're not dealing with eight-year-old little boys here, Frannie. These are grown men."

She sniffed, making him crazy.

"If there's one thing I've realized growing up in a household of nothing but brothers, Drew, it's that men never grow up. They're all little boys just hiding out in a man's body. It's the woman's cross to bear."

Drew stared at Frannie and wondered how much time he'd get for strangling her. If he'd just thought to start a tape recorder at the beginning of this ridiculous conversation, he'd probably get off scot-free. He took a deep, calming breath, exhaling through his nose. "Frannie, listen carefully. You cannot go around indiscriminately dispensing smiles as though they were candy."

Out of about eighty gabillion things Drew could have been upset about, this was the last thing Frannie would have expected. "I'm not supposed to smile at anyone, Drew? Have I got this right? You're mad because I *smiled* when you introduced me?"

"Don't look at me like I'm crazy," Drew began.

Frannie shrugged. Hey, if the shoe fit... "What would you like me to do? Scowl when I meet somebody? You don't think they'd think that was a little strange?"

Trust a woman to twist things around and make you look

foolish. Well not this time. He wasn't the one in the wrong here. "All I'm saying is that the kind of smile you were throwing around this morning could easily be misinterpreted."

Frannie let go of the pipe, settled her hand on a cocked hip. "And exactly how does one misinterpret a smile? It was a simple acknowledgment of an introduction."

Drew leaned close. "No. It was not. It was a come-on smile."

Eyes widened, Frannie's response was quick. "I don't think so!"

"It was." Drew nodded emphatically. "Want me to go back and ask the guys?"

"It was a hi-how-are-you smile," Frannie shot back hotly. "And even if Brian or Paul misinterpreted it, so what? That's how the game is played, isn't it? Let them know you're interested, they reciprocate, you go out a couple of times, see if there's anything in common and pursue the relationship or not from there, right?"

Drew swiped his hat off his head and threw it on the ground. "Oh, and tell me you could possibly be interested in Brian. Paul, maybe, he's not totally ugly. But Brian? Come on, Frannie. Don't waste your time trying to convince me you're attracted. He's a really nice guy, but there's not a woman alive willing to look past that kind of packaging. Like I said, he's a great guy but he's always had problems getting a woman. And now, after all the reading I've done I even know why."

"Oh, really?" Frannie crossed her arms and tapped her foot. "And just why is that, Dr. Lovelorn? Come on, fill me in. I can hardly wait to hear this."

"Well, even though we may not know it, we're evidently still operating on the same primitive instincts as we were a million or so years ago when it comes to attracting a mate."

Frannie thought about that. "This has something to do with the waist-to-hip ratio thing, doesn't it?"

Drew nodded. "Right. That ratio seemed to have a higher rate of successful childbirth. So a man would naturally seek that out in a mate. You know, taking steps to maximize the chances for the old survival-of-the-species kind of thing."

Frannie was doubtful. "Uh-huh. Right."

"Look, I don't have time to go into a lot of detail right now. I do have a company to run here. You're the one who asked me to look into this stuff. Trust me, I'm not making it up." He picked his hat up from the ground and whacked it on his thigh. Dust flew.

Frannie watched as he settled his cap back on his head. Man, had he always been so fidgety? "So what are you saying, Brian's waist-to-hip ratio is off?"

Drew rolled his eyes. "No, that's for girls, you know, for optimum chances of surviving childbirth. Would you just listen and let me get this out?"

Frannie stirred impatiently.

Drew put a finger on her lips. "Shhh. Just listen."

She had the strangest compulsion to lick his finger. *No, you're not interested in him any longer. He's a pretty boy. You don't need him. Think homely. Think grateful. Think adoring. Think pedestal.* Frannie almost snorted. If Drew ever put her on a pedestal and tried to adore her, she'd probably faint, fall off and break both legs and an arm.

Drew left his finger on her mouth, just to be safe. Besides, he found he liked touching her soft lips. Found he'd give just about anything if she'd open them up a bit, suck his finger inside, wrap her little pink tongue around it and... Drew barely refrained from groaning. Damn, he had to stop doing that. "Here's the thing, Frannie," he said, barely getting the words to form in his suddenly dry mouth. "Back in cave days a woman's and her children's survival de-

Silhouette ROMANCE® 1444
$3.50 U.S.
$3.99 CAN
M9

DIANA
PALMER

MERCENARY
WOMAN
SOLDIERS OF FORTUNE

We'd like to send you **2 FREE** books and a surprise gift to introduce you to Silhouette Romance®. Accept our special offer today and

Get Ready for a totally Refreshing Experience!

HOW TO QUALIFY:

1. With a coin, carefully scratch off the silver area on the card at right to see what we have for you—2 FREE BOOKS and a FREE GIFT—ALL YOURS! ALL FREE!

2. Send back the card and you'll receive two brand-new Silhouette Romance® novels. These books have a cover price of $3.99 each in the U.S. and $4.50 each in Canada, but they are yours to keep absolutely free!

3. There's no catch. You're under no obligation to buy anything. We charge nothing— ZERO—for your first shipment and you don't have to make any minimum number of purchases—not even one!

4. The fact is, thousands of readers enjoy receiving books by mail from the Silhouette Reader Service®. They enjoy the convenience of home delivery…they like getting the best new novels at discount prices, BEFORE they're available in stores…and they love their *Heart to Heart* subscriber newsletter featuring author news, horoscopes, recipes, book reviews and much more!

5. We hope that after receiving your free books you'll want to remain a subscriber. But the choice is yours—to continue or cancel, any time at all. So why not take us up on our invitation with no risk of any kind. You'll be glad you did!

SPECIAL FREE GIFT!

We can't tell you what it is…but we're sure you'll like it! A FREE gift just for giving the Silhouette Reader Service® a try!

Visit us at www.eHarlequin.com

The **2 FREE BOOKS** we send you will be selected from **SILHOUETTE ROMANCE®**, the series that brings you...a more traditional romance from first love to forever.

Books received may vary.

Scratch off the silver area to see what the Silhouette Reader Service has for you.

V *Silhouette*®
Where love comes alive™

YES! I have scratched off the silver area above. Please send me the **2 FREE** books and gift for which I qualify. I understand I am under no obligation to purchase any books, as explained on the back and on the opposite page.

315 SDL DH46   **215 SDL DH45**

FIRST NAME	LAST NAME

ADDRESS

APT.#	CITY

STATE/PROV.	ZIP/POSTAL CODE

Offer limited to one per household and not valid to current Silhouette Romance® subscribers. All orders subject to approval.

THE SILHOUETTE READER SERVICE®—Here's how it works:

Accepting your 2 free books and gift places you under no obligation to buy anything. You may keep the books and gift and return the shipping statement marked "cancel." If you do not cancel, about a month later we'll send you 6 additional books and bill you just $3.15 each in the U.S., or $3.50 each in Canada, plus 25¢ shipping & handling per book and applicable taxes if any.* That's the complete price and — compared to cover prices of $3.99 each in the U.S. and $4.50 each in Canada — it's quite a bargain! You may cancel at any time, but if you choose to continue, every month we'll send you 6 more books, which you may either purchase at the discount price or return to us and cancel your subscription.

*Terms and prices subject to change without notice. Sales tax applicable in N.Y. Canadian residents will be charged applicable provincial taxes and GST.

If offer card is missing write to: Silhouette Reader Service, 3010 Walden Ave., P.O. Box 1867, Buffalo NY 14240-1867

DETACH AND MAIL CARD TODAY!

BUSINESS REPLY MAIL
FIRST-CLASS MAIL   PERMIT NO. 717-003   BUFFALO, NY

POSTAGE WILL BE PAID BY ADDRESSEE

SILHOUETTE READER SERVICE
3010 WALDEN AVE
PO BOX 1867
BUFFALO NY 14240-9952

NO POSTAGE
NECESSARY
IF MAILED
IN THE
UNITED STATES

pended on her husband's strength. I mean, he had to go out and club a mastodon or two, then drag it home, right?"

"Mmmph."

He wasn't about to risk moving his finger, not with old motormouth here. He'd take that for agreement. "Right. So if he was a big guy with broad shoulders, good pecs, strong stomach muscles, why he'd be able to run down his prey, conk it over the head and still have enough muscle power left over to drag it home. To this day that's why women are attracted to that kind of guy. Why go for a wuss when King Kong'll keep you in the style you'd like to become accustomed to and last twice as long to boot, and that would be important since you didn't have the strength to hunt mastodons down for yourself? It's a survival kind of thing, okay? One of those things that got to be instinctual."

"Mmmph."

"Right. And remember when we did the digital camera thing? Cutting a picture of our faces in half and flip-flopping them to see if they were symmetrical?"

"Mmmph."

"Yes, well, same thing here. Even features, good skin were indicators of health, gave you a better chance of your mate still being around in a year or two instead of dying and leaving you with a couple of kids to scrounge around for. You try the symmetry test on old Bri back there and no matter how great a guy he is, I don't want to think about what you'd come up with." Drew shook his head. "No. A girl who looks like you, well, there's no way you could be attracted to him and I won't have you breaking his heart, hear me?"

Finally giving in to temptation, Frannie slipped her tongue out and licked his finger. It was warm, a little bit salty.

Drew jolted. His finger flew back, away from her mouth. Frannie poked him in the chest. "How dare you? Maybe *you* haven't progressed that far since cave days." She poked him harder. "In fact, being a *man,* I'm sure of it. I, on the other hand have risen above my hormones," she informed him loftily. "Just for your information, let me tell you I have decided purposely to look for somebody less than handsome." Frannie nodded fiercely. "Yes, I have."

Drew was incredulous. Would he ever understand the workings of the female mind? "You what?"

"You heard me. Women don't need a broad chest and major biceps in their man any more, and I, for one figured that out for myself. Okay, admittedly it was just last night, but hey, it's been eons, right? And a lot of other women still haven't figured out what I now see should be obvious." Frannie held up a hand to hold off any comment. "However, in their defense let me just say I'm expecting many of my sisters to follow suit shortly once they see how well I score here."

It was all he could do to refrain from throwing his cap on the ground again. "Frannie," Drew growled. "What in the name of all that's holy are you talking about?"

"King Kong, huh? Who would want him? Spends his time thumping his chest, his overly hairy chest, I might add, and carrying off unwilling women. Drew, you have just described the perfect alpha male."

"The what?" Frannie didn't like hairy men? Drew couldn't help but wonder how his own chest would score. He had hair there, sure, but he wouldn't exactly give King Kong a run for his money, at least not in that respect. He would call it, what? A moderately hairy cover. Yeah, that was it. Oh, never mind. Now she had him going all kinds of stupid, worrying about his chest hair. God, what next?

But Frannie was rolling now. "The thinking woman, of which I am one, will rise above centuries of sociological and genetic indoctrination, which I will. I've decided I want a beta male. Somebody in touch with their feminine side."

"Oh, my God." Drew sounded horrified. No one had ever accused him of being in touch with his feminine side, thank the Lord.

"Someone not afraid of their emotions, not afraid to share them."

"I'm about to hurl here."

"Someone who, when they look at me, sees more than a sex object."

"Oh, please." Drew was looking downright green now and conveniently forgetting how he'd felt when she'd described her bust measurements.

"And who's the most likely candidate to have done the introspection necessary to develop this kind of depth in their personality?" She didn't wait for Drew to respond, sure he'd never be able to figure it out for himself, being a complete idiot. Frannie held up a forefinger. "Who? Why the less than physically perfect male. The Brians of the world. They're the ones who will appreciate a good woman, since they're convinced they'll have to continue deferring to all you alphas and may have given up hope of getting a woman of their own."

Drew looked like he wanted to interrupt, but Frannie wasn't interested in anything he had to say. "No, I'm totally serious here. You ever listen to that oldies station, 94.3?"

He wasn't sure he wanted to admit to any such thing if it was going to help Frannie prove a no-doubt twisted point. "Yeah," he cautiously agreed.

"Did you ever hear that song, the one where the guy decides if he marries an ugly woman he's gonna be happy for the rest of his life and he's telling all his buddies to never marry a pretty one? That the ugly ones are better cooks, better everything? The assumption being the ugly woman has to try harder and the man gets a better deal with her."

"Frannie, it's just a song. It has no—"

"Yes or no, Drew? It's a simple yes-or-no question."

"Well, yeah, I'm familiar with the song."

"Okay," Frannie nodded. "So this is the same thing only in reverse. The sign of a good general is to constantly be willing to revise, not to cast your thinking in concrete," she pontificated. "This is my latest revision and I'm thinking it's a good one. I want somebody ugly." She paused, thought. Ugly might be going a bit too far. She had to look at him across the breakfast table, after all. All right, so, "Homely, at any rate. I figure they'll try harder to make me happy since I was willing to look past the surface. I will be equally grateful to be married to someone so kind and thoughtful. The lucky guy will have no regrets, I will make sure of that. He's gonna think he's died and gone to nirvana.

"Think about it, Drew, that's all I ask. It's brilliant."

Drew stared as if she'd grown another head. "You are so strange." He shook his head and turned to walk away but stopped after a few steps and looked back. "You know," he said, "Darwin and all the other scientists were wrong with all their natural selection and their survival of the fittest stuff. You know how I know that, Frannie? Because you're the living proof. Your mind is the product of millions of years of natural selection? I don't think so." And he walked off and left her.

Frannie grinned at his retreating back and brushed off her hands. It hadn't been too hard to shake loose from Drew. And everything she'd said had been the truth, Drew just hadn't wanted to hear it, being one of the beautiful people of the world. Her smile firmly in place and a bounce in her step, Frannie went off in search of the nearest homely guy. Upon finding him, she would promptly offer her help in...whatever.

She ran into Paul Campbell instead.

"Hey," he said.

"Hay is for horses," Frannie promptly responded. "But hey, yourself."

White teeth flashed in his reddish-gold beard. "How's it going so far?"

Sticking her hands in her coverall pockets and rocking on her feet, Frannie responded, "So far so good. What're you up to?"

"Me? I'm gonna go load me a truck, lift heavy stuff and grunt. You want to watch?"

Happily, Frannie fell into step beside him. "Sure. I'll even help. How'd your painting turn out? You must be good, huh? You got done awfully fast." He was an artist. Artists were sensitive people, good with their hands, weren't they? Sensitive, deft hands just might outweigh the fact that he was, while not in Drew's same category, still a pretty darn decent-looking guy.

Could that possibly make him the best of both worlds?

Hmm, well, only one way to find out.

"I'm waiting for my wash to dry," Paul said leading his way back to a different warehouse.

"Oh?" Frannie followed. She was confused. "I didn't know you could do laundry here. What did you get dirty?"

Paul laughed. "No. I laid down a watercolor wash. It's got to dry before I paint anything else on top of it or the paint will bleed."

Frannie nodded knowledgeably. "Oh. Sure. Um, you said your paint was going to bleed? Not like blood, though, right?" Man, was this guy even talking the same language? Maybe he wasn't such a good choice after all.

"Not like blood," Paul assured her as he held the door to the greenhouse open for her. He grabbed a cart and began pushing it down the aisle.

Frannie trailed behind, impressed once more with all the greenery surrounding her. Drew was responsible for all this.

Talk about your green thumb. Talk about your visionary capabilities. Man, Drew had them in spades. And he was making it all work. All she had to do was look around to see that. Darn, she would not think about him. Frannie hurried to catch up with Paul. "You were saying?" she said.

"Hmm? Oh, if I paint another layer while the first one's still wet, the paint will spread all over and I won't get a nice crisp edge, see? It'll blur. When that happens you say the paint bled."

"Ah. Bleeding paint. And we wouldn't want that." They'd come to a stop. Frannie took the peat pots Paul handed her and arranged them neatly on the push cart.

"Depends," Paul said. He stopped, pointed at the plants on the cart and silently mouthed numbers, obviously doing a mental tally on what he'd collected so far. "It all depends on what I'm doing. There is such a thing as painting wet on wet with watercolors. I used that technique when I was laying down the wash. You do that when you want the colors to run together. Makes for some nice variation in your tone. But now I want to do wet on dry so I've got to be patient and wait."

"Uh-huh, sure. Wet on wet, wet on dry. I get it." No she didn't. So she'd get a book after work and read up on it. "You get seventy-two? I counted seventy-two."

Paul nodded. "Yeah. We'll probably need three, four times that amount. But right now I want to get a feel for the project first. Give the customer an idea of what it's going to look like. We'll start off with two to three per square yard. They'll probably come back and have us up it to four to six. We'll see. So, you're Drew's friend's little sister, huh?"

"Yeah, I'm Rick's sister. His all-grown-up, totally legal younger sister." Frannie followed Paul down the aisle. Somehow it was going to be a problem that she was related to Drew's friend. She could sense it. "You ever meet him?" Frannie asked.

"Who?"

"Rick."

"Oh. Yeah. Couple of times. I don't really know him or anything, but yeah, I met him."

"Nice guy."

"Seemed to be." Paul started handing her plants again.

"But he's my brother, not my father."

"Uh-huh."

But to Frannie, Paul didn't sound convinced. She sighed as she stacked. This could turn out to be a long summer. "What are these?"

"You'd probably call them bulrushes. They're real good for areas with high BOD."

Frannie had been taking night classes since she'd graduated from college. She was halfway to a master's degree. She was not a stupid person. So how come she felt so dumb? "BOD? What's that? There were some guys, Alpha Sigs we met at a fraternity party one time that I thought had pretty hot bods, and there's always George Clooney, but somehow I don't think we're talking about the same thing here."

"Not exactly. BOD stands for the biochemical oxygen demand. Wastewater with high BOD needs a lot of oxygen moved into it to get it stabilized. The old Soil Conservation Service which is now the Natural Resources Conservation Service has done a lot of studies on this stuff. They recommend emergent plants, the kind that grow above the water, as the best for moving a lot of oxygen into the roots and out into the water. In other words, we'll be planting a lot of reeds, bulrushes and cattails all summer."

If he said so. "Okay."

Paul looked at her, scratched his beard. "Drew's a pretty good guy."

"I'm sure he is."

"I wouldn't want to step on his toes."

"I think his boots are steel-tipped. I don't think you have to worry."

"I've never before seen him act like he was this morning."

Oh, like an idiot? But Frannie didn't say that, even though she wanted to. It was important to remain professional. And a professional person did not cut down their boss to another employee. However, wait until she got home. Her little one-story's walls were going to get an earful. "Oh? I'm not sure what you mean by that."

Paul shrugged. "He wasn't himself," he said and shrugged again. "He seemed kind of agitated, abrupt."

"Really? And that's unusual for him?" It seemed fairly typical to her. At least whenever he was around Frannie.

"Yeah. It is. He's usually Mr. Calm. Very even-tempered."

You'd have to prove it by her.

"Okay," said Paul. "Let's come at this from another angle. You know those Alpha Sigs you mentioned earlier?"

Frannie straightened a six pack of peat pots. "What about them?"

"I was just wondering. Drew. How would you categorize him? Is he hot?"

Frannie rearranged a few more pots while she thought. How the heck did she answer that? There was a trapdoor waiting at the end of any response she could give. Oh, well, she'd never been much good at lying. And the fact that she'd gotten past all that surface-attraction stuff didn't mean she wasn't aware of the packaging anymore. Come on, she wasn't blind after all, just in total control of her pheromones. "Yes," she admitted to Paul, to herself. "Drew's a hottie. He's got a darn good bod. And I'm not talking about oxygen demand here.'' And she wasn't interested in his bod. Not even a little bit. Drew could keep his body *and* his oxygen demands.

Yeah, right.

Evidently Paul was on the same wave length. ''Uh-huh. That's what I was afraid of. I think he's interested, too.''

''No, you're wrong about that.'' Frannie was sure about that.

''I don't think so.''

''No, really. You are. He's totally commitment-phobic, and while I admit to a bit of a crush once upon a time, I'm over it. Totally, completely over it.''

Paul's ''Uh-huh,'' sounded anything but sure.

Frannie shook her hair back. ''I'm serious. Really. There's nothing between us.'' She helped him push the cart when it caught on a stick.

Paul considered her words then nodded to himself. ''Okay. I'll go see if it's all right for you to come along to the site. It might be interesting for you. Not really before-and-after kind of thing because there's been a lot of preparation work done already, but close enough.''

Frannie grinned. ''Sounds good. I can load some of this stuff onto the truck while you do that. Earn my keep.''

Paul nodded his approval. ''Get Amos to help you. He should be back there somewhere. Big guy. No neck. He used to play football,'' Paul said by way of explanation for the missing neck.

''Will he know which truck we should use?''

''He should.''

Paul helped Frannie get the loaded cart through the greenhouse doorway then went off in search of Drew.

He found him in his office, scowling over some papers. Paul knocked on the open door frame. ''Hey.''

Glancing up, Drew's scowl remained. ''What?''

''Mark called. They're ready to start some planting. I'm

going to run a truckload over there. Is it okay if Frannie rides along so she can see what we do?''

Drew's scowl deepened. "Didn't take long to get on a first-name basis, did it?''

Paul's brow rose. "We're all on a first-name basis around here, Drew. It's your company, you know that. Heck, you started the policy. You want I should call her Miss Parker? Gonna sound damn odd.''

"Oh, shut up." In his hands was a contract. One Drew wanted very badly. So how come he was itching to crush it and pretend it was Paul's head? Drew shook his own head hoping to clear it. Damn it, he liked Paul. Or at least he had up until about an hour or so ago. And he needed Paul. Nobody rendered a drawing like Paul. The problem was right now, Drew didn't care much for anybody. The life of a hermit was starting to sound real good to him.

This was Frannie's fault. Had to be. Drew had always felt the most fortunate of men. If Wiseman Environmental was his job, it was also his place of refuge. Not many men were so fortunate. He loved his work. No life of quiet desperation for him, no sir.

So how come he wanted nothing more than to back the day up and start it all over again? He would take the day off, pick up Frannie and run to some other corner of the earth with her, introducing her to exactly nobody.

"Listen, Paul, it's only been a couple of weeks since you broke up with Jenny and while Frannie is as cute as can be, I just think—''

"You *are* interested. I thought so. You've been acting weird all morning. Well, not to worry. I'll step back and—''

Drew picked up a pencil and dropped it on his desk. "I am *not* interested.'' He made a sweeping gesture. "Be my guest. Consider the field clear. My only point was—''

"You're sure? Hey, man, I don't want to poach on your territory. I owe you a lot, after all."

Leaning forward in his chair, Drew pointed his index finger at Paul. "I am not interested, okay? Not interested. I just worry that you may be acting on the rebound, you know? I don't want you hurt, okay? And while I'm not *interested* interested in Frannie, I do care for her. You know, in a big-brotherly kind of way." Yeah, right. Drew ground his teeth together.

"Gotcha. Big brother."

"Yes. Like that. For reasons unknown, she's suddenly all hot to get married. Women and their biological clocks." Drew snorted. "Who can figure? The point being, I don't want her hurt either. Not either one of you. I just think maybe you should see Jenny one more time. Make sure it's really over."

"I don't think so. And we're both adults here, Drew."

Drew picked up the pencil and threw it again. "So Frannie has repeatedly assured me."

"Maybe you should listen."

Grimacing, Drew remarked, "Like I have a choice."

Paul grinned. "Oh, you've got a choice, old buddy. I believe in personal accountability. Say the word and I'm out. You hear me? Gone."

Oh, he wanted to say the word, he really did. The question was, why? Frannie was twenty-four. The proof was irrefutable. There was no damn basis for his protective feelings anymore. None.

Except chronological age didn't always equate to experience, and Frannie taught second grade, for God's sake. The eight-year-old boy didn't bear a whole lot of resemblance to the mature male of the species. Oh, damn. What to do?

"Just don't hurt her," Drew finally admonished. "I'd have to break your neck then."

"Hey, we're going out to throw a few plants in the ground, that's all. I'll bring her back in one piece, promise."

Yeah, right, one piece, Drew thought as he stared at the now-empty door frame. Heart included?

And that was pretty much how the rest of that week and the next went.

The weather was beautiful. Perfect for planting. Drew got that big contract signed, sealed and delivered. He'd had several more calls for estimates. He was in the position of possibly having to turn down some jobs. It didn't get much better than that.

There was only one fly in the ointment.

Every single one of his men was in love with Frannie.

He didn't understand it, and Drew had given it a lot of thought. His word choice had been deliberate. They weren't in lust with her, which he could have understood intellectually when he took into account her better-than-average breasts and her sixty-five percent waist-to-hip ratio. No, they *loved* her, which as nearly as Drew could figure was some kind of combination of lusting and genuine caring.

According to the reports he got back, she was hot, but mostly they just liked her. She was unfailingly kind to everybody—even the maintenance guy who could probably scare a corpse back to life, he was so homely. Frannie was open and genuine, they said. She pitched in wherever and whenever, coming back every bit as mucky and dirty as the rest of them. And all the while, she never lost an ounce of her femininity. They adored her, plain and simple. No one had asked her out because they'd put her on some kind of pedestal where they worshipped but didn't feel worthy to touch. And besides, these were all nice guys worried about stepping on each other's toes.

Drew wondered how long that would last. Chaos and enmity was sure to break out at any moment. Everything he'd worked so hard to build up could be destroyed. Worse, Drew felt like an outsider in his own company, because all Frannie's smiles and joie de vivre seemed to be reserved for the guys who worked for him. It was an odd sensation, being left at the starting blocks *because* of his looks. Not that he wanted to be in the running, because most assuredly he didn't. No, it was just disconcerting, that was all.

But she had certainly proved her point. Frannie wasn't interested in his money or his looks the way most women, at least the ones of his acquaintance were. Heck, even if he decided to go after her, he wouldn't have a hook to use. He didn't understand her. Not at all.

Friday morning, he cornered her as she prepared to hop on to a truck pulling out of the lot on its way to a site.

"Frannie, wait."

She tugged her cap on. "What?"

"You're coming to the rehearsal dinner tonight for Rick and Evie, right?"

"So?"

"I'll pick you up. Six o'clock. And I can take you to the wedding tomorrow, too."

Frannie looked at Drew oddly. "I guess. Okay. I didn't ask anyone special, I was going by myself anyway. It'll save me some gas."

Drew nodded, oddly relieved. "Right. I didn't ask a date, either. Didn't want Rick and Evie to have to pay for an extra plate. We'll carpool."

"See you at six, then."

"Yeah, six." He watched the truck pull out of the lot. Six. Now why had he done that?

Chapter Seven

"So, Keith, you met Evie back in high school?"

"Yes, that's right. We were in a play together. *Peter Pan*. I was Nana. The dog?"

"Frannie?" Drew interrupted.

"Just a second, Drew." Frannie smiled up at one of the groomsmen she'd just met. "Who did Evie play?"

"Oh, she was Wendy. I was really jealous. She got to fly while I was earthbound and did nothing but bark."

"Frannie, I—"

She held up a hand in Drew's direction. "She really flew? How'd they pull that off?"

"The school actually hired a professional company to come in with the wires and all the rest of the equipment we needed to pull it off. They stayed for a week and trained the crew how to use it all, too. It cost a small fortune, but you should have seen the looks on the kids' faces in the audience when Peter and Wendy took off into the air."

"I bet. I—"

"Frannie, I hate to interrupt, but—"

No he didn't. He'd been doing it consistently, every time she started a conversation with someone. Especially a male someone. "Drew, what is the matter with you? You've been acting odd all night. Is there something wrong?"

"It's getting late, Frannie. Don't you have an early appointment to get your hair and makeup done?"

"Ten o'clock isn't all that early, Drew." Frannie checked her wristwatch. "And it's only eleven-thirty. It's not like I'm going to turn into a pumpkin or anything. Aren't you enjoying yourself?"

No, as a matter of fact, he wasn't enjoying himself. Not that he'd admit any such thing to Frannie. Some of Evie's bridesmaids were darn good-looking women with no sign of anything significant on their left hand. But instead of feeling like he was in heaven, Drew felt as though he'd been dropped into hell as he watched Frannie being personable, making sure she spoke to everyone in the room. Did she have to be so darn friendly? Every male in the place probably thought she was coming on to him the way she was dispensing smiles so freely.

And that was totally unfair and he knew it. Man, he really disliked this new side of himself he was suddenly manifesting. He could be a real jerk. Who'd have thought it?

"Listen, Drew, I can catch a ride with—"

No! He'd brought her, he'd take her home. "Frannie, you've been up since five. You've got to be tired. You won't be able to enjoy the day tomorrow or look your best if you don't get some sleep tonight."

Frannie excused herself. "I'm sorry, Keith. It looks like my ride is ready to leave."

Keith's eyes shifted between Frannie and Drew and back again. Clearly, he was trying to figure out the dynamics of their relationship. "I'll see you tomorrow?"

Frannie smiled. "I'll look forward to it." She let Drew

hustle her away. As soon as they were out of earshot, she hissed between clenched teeth, "What is your problem? Tell me you're sick. Tell me you've had too much to drink and need me to drive. Tell me something so I don't continue thinking you're an absolute idiot."

That could be tough considering that was exactly how he felt. "You'll thank me come tomorrow."

"I don't think so. Drew, I was making progress. That Keith guy liked me. I could tell."

"Yeah, well, that might be true. He might've liked you. But you didn't like him."

Incensed, Frannie exploded. "What? How do you know I didn't like him? *I* don't even know if I liked him or not, you dragged me out of there before I could find out much about him."

"Trust me, your body language was an open book."

She stopped in the middle of the parking lot. "And just what's that supposed to mean? What about my body language? What was wrong with my body language, for crying out loud?"

"You want to talk about this right here and now? In the parking lot? Fine. Okay. Keith is a snake—"

"Keith a snake..." Frannie was temporarily bereft of words. "You haven't spoken more than two words to the man. How can you possibly know if he's a snake or not? You know what? I think you better hand over the keys to the car. I think you've had too much to drink. And if you're not drunk you've gone completely mental. Either way I'm not getting into a car with you behind the wheel."

"Don't be ridiculous, I—" He took in her stubborn look and threw up his hands. "All right, okay, I'm sorry. My mistake. Keith might not be a snake." That was as much as Drew was willing to allow; he still wasn't convinced. "And he was interested in you, I'll give you that."

"Oh, well thank you very much."

"No, seriously. Did you notice the way he was standing? His feet were pointed directly at you and his—"

Frannie rolled her eyes. "Here we go again. Body language. Man, you read one book and suddenly you're an expert. Ever hear the saying a little knowledge is a dangerous thing, Drew? Ever wonder how sayings get to be sayings, hmm?"

"If you don't want to hear this, fine," Drew responded stiffly and started off again. Where the heck had he parked his car? Usually he drove the truck and it stuck up over the tops of the other vehicles. He'd gotten out of the habit of having to remember where he parked as he could usually pick it out right away. It was hard to stomp off when you didn't know which direction to go. Think, man, think. Let's see…oh, yeah. Doing an about-face, Drew led the way to the car.

"Don't want to hear it? *Don't want to hear it?*" Frannie squawked, her heels clicking on the blacktop of the parking lot as she followed in hot pursuit. "Oh don't be silly, Drew. I'm dying to hear this. Why, I'm waiting with bated breath."

Finally they stood beside his car. Thank God. "Get in," he ordered stiffly.

She glared at him. "Not until you tell me what you meant."

"Oh for God's sake, fine! You had your arms crossed over your chest, all right? It was a dead giveaway."

"My arms were crossed? That's it?"

"Yes, that's it. Your arms were crossed. It's a very defensive position, for your information. You were not open to his advances, in fact, you were blocking him."

Frannie threw her hands up in exasperation then pulled her car door open and slid in. "Get in and start the car, will you? It's really cooled down. I'm cold."

"Try wearing clothes. You'd be amazed how much warmer you'd be."

"I am wearing clothes. And don't you dare criticize my dress. I got a lot of compliments tonight."

Drew dropped behind the wheel of the car and gave her dress a disparaging glance. "There's not enough of that thing to call it a dress. What, we're in a recession? Dressmakers can't afford fabric? Hemlines do go up every time the economy gets into trouble, you know. How much did you pay for that, anyway?"

Frannie drew in an insulted breath and almost popped out of her admittedly scooped-lower-than-she-usually-scooped neckline. Drew had a difficult time taking his eyes off her chest long enough to safely back out of his parking space.

"None of your business what I paid." A lot. She'd wanted to impress him. "And as of this moment, I am no longer speaking to you. Oh, by the way, I'll drive myself tomorrow."

Drew gunned the car out onto the street and grunted. "Typical woman. Follows up her vow not to speak with another comment. And I'll be picking you up. Rick asked me to. He wants you at Evie's by nine o'clock. Besides, you'll need help carrying all your junk."

What junk? Frannie wanted to ask but managed to bite her tongue. Her dress, shoes and a little makeup bag. Big deal. She would not lower herself to argue with him, however. She'd simply be gone by the time he got there. Frannie turned her head and watched the houses whiz by, ignoring Drew. Arrogant male.

"Your muscles are going to be all stiff, and you won't be able to enjoy yourself tomorrow if you don't relax," Drew informed her as he walked her up her sidewalk.

"More body language?" Frannie asked, breaking her

vow of silence again. "My arms aren't crossed over my chest, Drew."

"Maybe not, but you've definitely got a pole down your back and your knuckles have gone white from clenching your fists. I think I'd prefer the crossed arms. Right now you look ready to slug me."

Oh, the temptation was strong, the know-it-all.

Drew took her key right out of her hand and unlocked the front door. He pushed it open and walked in in front of Frannie. "Wait right here," he ordered and left her just inside the front door while he checked through the small living room, kitchen and bedroom. He even peered into the bathroom before he was satisfied there were no prowlers lurking.

"Don't you want to check under the bed?" Frannie inquired nastily, tapping her foot but refusing to cross her arms over her chest.

"Everything looks okay," Drew grunted, not allowing himself to be baited.

"What do you think I do when you're not around, Drew? I go in and out of this place on a fairly regular basis, you know."

"Well I'm here tonight, aren't I? So tonight it gets checked over before I leave."

"My hero."

"Shut up, Frannie." And he knew one way to do it for sure. He grabbed her, folded her into his arms and kissed the breath right out of her.

"Mmmph."

"Mmm."

There'd been lemon sorbet for dessert and that was exactly how Frannie tasted. Tart. Citrussy. Delicious. His tongue ran along the seam of her closed lips.

Drew must have had an after-dinner coffee. She could even tell that there'd been cream and sugar in it. Her arms wrapped around his neck and Frannie rose up on tiptoe to better meet his marauding mouth. Darn, but she hated that he was such a good kisser. Why couldn't he just leave her alone so she could get over this infatuation? But nooo, not Drew. When had he ever done anything the easy way?

Frannie parted her lips and let Drew's tongue slip inside the warmth of her mouth. At the same time she noticed that he'd spread his legs, probably for balance, but the effect was that Frannie was now tucked right up next to him.

The man was hot. Red hot. And the proof was prodding her right in the stomach.

Life is so unfair.

It was her final coherent thought. Drew's tongue danced around hers. It licked playfully at hers. Then it dropped the play and got serious. Drew sucked Frannie's tongue right into his own mouth and Frannie's breathing about stopped.

That kind of intensity can't be maintained too awfully long without killing one or both parties, or so Frannie believed. Just when she reached the breathe-or-pass-out point, Drew finally pulled back. He rested his forehead on hers as they both sucked in much-needed oxygen.

"Damn," he said.

Yeah. Frannie agreed with the sentiment.

"The University of Chicago could have saved themselves a whole bunch of research and time if you'd been around during World War II, babe," he said.

Frannie was still inhaling deeply, trying to catch her breath. "What?" she managed to get out.

"Little Boy. Big Boy. Little Big Boy. Whatever the name of that first atomic bomb was. Little girl, you could have taken it, hands down."

"Thank you. I think."

"No prob." Drew took in a large steadying breath. "Okay, well, that was certainly a mistake. I'm sorry, okay?

I apologize. I'll, uh, pick you up at eight forty-five, baby. Be ready." And with a little salute, he was gone.

Frannie locked her door, then leaned against it while she waited for her leg muscles to firm up and do their job. He'd apologized for kissing her. *Apologized.* The jerk. *Baby?* Drew had never called her baby before. And just exactly what had he meant about a mistake?

Sighing, she took a deep breath and pushed off from the door. She made it to the coffee table and from there to the hallway. The hallway had a chair rail and Frannie ran her hand along it, just in case, as she made her way to the bathroom. She needed a cool shower to clear her head. Evidently, that one glass of champagne had hit much harder than she'd thought.

Frannie had trouble falling asleep that night with the result that when she did finally drop off, she slept hard. So hard, in fact, that she slept through her alarm. It was eight twenty-eight when Frannie groggily opened one eye and peered at the bedside clock.

"Oh, my God," she breathed and flew out of bed.

So much for being gone when Drew came to fetch her. She'd be lucky if she only kept him waiting a little while. Little while, she mused. Where had that expression come from, anyway? And what was it's opposite, a lot of while? *Never mind, Frannie, just hurry!*

Pulling a T-shirt on over her head, Frannie stepped into a clean pair of the jean coveralls she'd come to love since working for Drew, only these were short length. She pulled the straps up over her shoulders and hitched them both. None of this leaving one side undone for her. The object was to hang onto your pants, after all.

Blindly searching under the bed with a hand, she found first one, then the other tennis shoe and slipped her feet into them. "He's going to be here any minute," Frannie mumbled as she hurriedly tied the second shoelace. And

Drew did not like to be kept waiting. She'd known that since she was twelve years old. "Darn, darn, darn. Where is my hairbrush? Okay, I remember I used it last night right here in the bedroom and then I set it down...where? My hair looks like I stuck my finger into an electrical outlet. Oh, damn, there's the doorbell. He's here."

Frannie answered the door looking like a wild woman. "Hi."

Drew looked her up and down. His brow rose. "What took you so long? I was starting to think something was wrong and that maybe I should kick the door in, make sure you weren't hurt or anything."

Then again, it might have been a good thing she'd slept late. At least she was here to protect her door. "The alarm didn't go off. Either that or I turned it off in my sleep."

Drew nodded wisely. "I told you—"

"Don't go there, Drew. Just don't."

He rocked on his heels. "Okaaay. We're in a good mood. Uh, Frannie? Your hair is very...big this morning."

Frannie touched her head self-consciously. "It's called bedhead. I couldn't find my hairbrush, all right? Now how about helping me carry some of this stuff so we can go?"

Bedhead? Well didn't that just bring to mind all kinds of mental imagery. Especially with Frannie looking all sleep-rumpled and sloe-eyed. Drew cleared his throat. "Uh, sure. What would you like me to take?"

Thrusting her plastic-bagged bridesmaid dress at him, Frannie said, "Here. Take this. I can handle the rest of it."

Without quibbling, Drew took the proffered dress and followed Frannie down the sidewalk, humming under his breath. He could have handled more, but with Frannie occupied juggling the rest of her things she was distracted enough to not notice Drew admiring her rear view and her surprisingly sexy big hair. Shortalls, or whatever they were called were hard on a man's heart. He could feel his own pumping double-time as he took in the long length of trim leg the whacked-off coveralls left exposed.

"Your legs are too long," he groused as he helped Frannie into his car. "Heck, you're so short, you don't need such long legs. They're out of proportion."

She gave him a superior look. "They're barely long enough to reach the ground. You'll notice there's nothing left over."

Drew rolled his eyes and didn't speak again until they'd reached Evie's place.

Frannie leaned forward and stared out the windshield as Drew pulled in to the curb. "Wow," she said. "Look at that stretch limo. I didn't know they came that long. But they're awfully early. Evie's going to be upset if they start charging from now. He wasn't supposed to come until it was time to go to the church."

Smiling smugly, Drew explained, "The limo's a surprise for Evie. Rick called and changed the order to the bigger one. He also upped the time. The driver is at you girls' disposal for the entire day. The limo's waiting to take you all to the hairdresser's."

With eyes grown big, Frannie responded, "Really? Wow. I wonder if Evie's noticed it yet. I've known Rick my entire life and I never would have guessed…hurry up, Drew. I want to see Evie's face when she gets a load of this." Arms laden, Frannie hurried up the walk. "This is just so romantic."

Drew rolled his eyes again. Romantic? Corny, if you asked him. Still, Rick seemed to have called it. It wouldn't hurt to take notes, but it didn't seem right to play on a woman's gullibility like that.

"Did you see the limousine out front?" Evie squealed the moment she opened the door in answer to Frannie's ring. "It's ours for the whole day, not just to the church and the reception, the whole day! Can you believe it? Isn't Rick the best ever?''

Considering Frannie had found him a brotherly thorn in her side for as long as she could remember, Frannie figured it just might be time to reevaluate Rick. Really, who'd have thought? "Yes, I guess he is," she said. At the very least, he'd come a long way, baby. Frannie eyed Drew thoughtfully. Was there hope? She took in the disgusted look on his face. Nah.

Drew dumped Frannie's stuff in the foyer, turned around and left the women in Evie's front vestibule gushing over Rick's romantic nature.

"What a crock," he muttered, then snorted, "romantic, my foot. He's just trying to rack up brownie points. And look at them fall for it hook, line and sinker. Master manipulator, that's my buddy Rick. I just pray to God I never sink so low, that's all. A man should have some pride." Drew dropped behind the wheel of his car and drove off, intent on finding something guy to do until he was forced to put on the tux and the green cummerbund and get to the church.

"...And then, when everybody was there? We all got into the limo and you'll never guess what."

Probably not, but Drew imagined he'd have to make a stab at it or be branded a slug...or worse. The wedding was a done deal. Rick and Evie were married. A dinner had been served to the obnoxious sound of guests beating their spoons and forks on their water glasses so the happy couple would kiss, which they had done any number of times and now the band was playing a slow dance at the reception. In his arms was Frannie. Unfortunately, she felt like she was made to fit there. She seemed able to follow him effortlessly and the few glimpses he caught in the mirrors along the wall told him they made a good-looking couple out on the dance floor.

He sighed. His mother had been right after all. The infamous *someday* had come, but darned if he was going to call her up and thank her for making him take dance lessons.

"Drew, are you listening?"

"Hmm? Oh, sure, Frannie. Uh, what'd you guys find in the limousine?" Oh, on a wild guess, let's see, "Champagne? Chocolates?"

"Only it was white chocolate," Frannie gushed, "so that once she had her dress on it wouldn't get stained. Can you believe my brother thought of that?"

"Frankly, no."

"And a white rose with a note telling her how happy he was that today had finally come." Frannie sighed. "I can't believe this is the same guy who put a frog in my bed."

"It wasn't real." And he had been the one to talk Rick into the prank when they'd seen it at the store.

"Doesn't matter," Frannie said with a shudder. "It looked real. My mom made him play Barbies with me all afternoon the next day."

Rick had given him a bloody nose for that. "Yes, well, you were saying?" Hard to believe Frannie had actually found a subject he wanted to talk about even less than Rick's pathetic attempts at romanticism, but there you were. He guided her through a turn.

Wouldn't you know Drew would be a smooth dancer? How come she hadn't known about that? His biceps were firm under her hand, his hand on her back intimate. He'd removed his jacket and it was obvious Drew wore no undershirt. She could see the outline of the small bronze discs of his nipples and the sprinkling of firm chest hair pushing against his shirt. It was all Frannie could do to refrain from laying her head on his broad chest. Who could care about proper dance posture when Drew had you in his arms? Obviously, a stronger woman than Frannie, that was for sure.

"Frannie?"

"Hmm? Oh, right. So, anyway, when we got to the beauty shop, Rick had called ahead and made arrangements for a full body massage for Evie. On the massage table was another rose with a note saying he wanted her relaxed for her big day." Frannie sighed again.

So did Drew. "Romantic," he said with a sad but knowledgeable nod.

"Man. I just hope there's another guy like him somewhere out there for me. But I've got to tell you, after today I think it's really going to take some looking."

"So what else did Mr. Romance do?" Might as well get the litany over and done with, Drew figured morosely. He'd had no idea his buddy Rick could be so sneaky.

"The beautician pulled a rose out of her table drawer when she was done with Evie. That note said he didn't need to see her to know she looked beautiful. She always looked good to him."

Sappy, really sappy. But effective, evidently. He could hear it in Frannie's voice, and she hadn't even been the recipient. Drew blew out some air. "Any more roses after that?"

"Oh, yeah."

Of course. He should have known. Drew spun Frannie into a pirouette, then hauled her back in close.

"The lady who did her nails gave her one, then there was another one on the seat of the limo again. And listen to this—"

Frannie's hair smelled like a ripe orchard. It was even bigger than when he'd dropped her off at Evie's. The itch to bury his face in it was really, really strong. It was so unfair. "What?"

Frannie inhaled discreetly. Drew's aftershave was subtle,

but awfully darn effective. It certainly had her attention. "Yes, well, the driver didn't bring us straight back to Evie's."

"He took a detour? Where to?"

"By that fancy lingerie shop downtown."

Now that had potential. "Yeah?"

"Yes. He honked the horn and the manager came out and handed Evie a box tied up in ribbon and—"

Drew nodded. He was getting the pattern here. "A white rose."

"I couldn't see what was in the box. Evie shut it too fast after she opened it, but I can imagine. She blushed really hard. I did see the card attached to the rose, though. Something about a fun wedding night for both of them, I can't remember exactly."

"So how many are we up to? Four? Is that it?"

"No. It was unbelievable. Every time we turned around, somebody was whipping out a rose and handing it to her. There was even one in her refrigerator when Evie went to get the luncheon out. She ended up with a full dozen by the time we found a few more in the bridal dressing room in the back of church. Oh, and the best part?"

He took her into a promenade. She followed perfectly. Damn. "What? What was the best part?"

"Well, we were all going to carry just a single rose. To save money, you know? But in the back of the church, the florist was there, waiting. She had baby's breath, greenery and ribbon with her. She took all the roses and made that bouquet Evie carried right there, five minutes before she walked down the aisle. She even incorporated all the cards into it. Wasn't it beautiful?"

Reluctantly, Drew agreed. "Yeah, it was nice."

"Evie said she was going to dry the bouquet and save it forever."

That did it. Drew shook his head. "See, that's what I

don't get about women. What's she want with a bunch of old dead flowers? What's she going to do with them?''

"Remember her wedding day, which my brother has made sure was any woman's dream?''

"Whatever. Isn't that why you pay a small fortune for a photographer? How many reminders do you need, for God's sake?'' He gestured to his shirt. ''Who'd want to remember these monkey suits, anyway?''

Frannie came to a dead halt in the middle of the dance floor. ''You know what your problem is?''

Reluctantly Drew dropped his hands. He already missed the feel of her. ''I can hardly wait. What's my problem?''

"You haven't got a romantic bone in your body, that's your problem. You're never going to get married.''

Well finally, some good news.

"No woman will put up with you. That's why you're always dating somebody different. The packaging is great, but there's nothing solid underneath.''

Drew had seen firsthand how a marriage degenerated once the sexual hum was gone. His parents had been a prime example. There'd been nothing but bickering and resentment in the end. ''That's complete baloney. If I wanted to be saddled with a wife and kids, I could do it, just like that.'' He snapped his fingers. Drew all but dragged her off to the side. ''But let me tell you this, little girl. Guys...and girls too...they mistake sexual attraction for this nebulous thing called love. They're in lust, but that's not a politically correct term at the moment, so they convince themselves it's *love*.'' He said the word the way you'd say *plague* or *STD*.

Frannie put her hands on her hips. She didn't back up one bit. ''Oh, really?''

"Yes, really. But tell you what, five years from now when those two have two or three little ones, they're exhausted from sitting up with the baby all night, the older ones have the chicken pox, they haven't had sex in a month because the baby's still sleeping in their bed and they're too damn tired the few times they're actually alone, well then they're going to remember this day and wonder what the heck they'd been thinking of.''

"You're crazy."

"No. I'm a realist. I keep my relationships casual because I know how they're going to end otherwise. Like my parents. I can be just as *romantic*—" he said it like a dirty word "—as Rick on my worst day, but I won't do that to a woman. I won't do it to myself."

Frannie stared at him. "I feel sorry for you," she finally said.

"Don't." Drew pursed his lips. "Here. I'll prove it to you."

Hands on her hips, Frannie archly inquired, "How?"

"You remember my sister? Karen?"

"Sort of. She was a lot older than you."

"Only five years." Drew shrugged. "Probably seemed like a lot at the time. Anyway, she's been married eight years and guess what? She says her marriage is tired and their relationship needs *renewing,* whatever that means. They're taking a long weekend away. My mom is getting too old for twenty-four-hour days with the three little hellions so I got hornswaggled into watching the monsters."

"I'm sorry your sister and her husband are having trouble. But that doesn't mean—"

"I want you to come with me. Help me watch them. At the end of the weekend, tell me your biological clock is still ringing. Hell, all you're going to want to do is push the sleep button, roll over and pull the covers up over your head. I know."

Frannie snorted. "Oh, you do, do you?"

"Yes. As a matter of fact, if I'm wrong and you still want to get married and produce your own little monsters,

I'll marry you myself." Why didn't the idea terrify him the way it should? Well, no matter, it would never happen.

Frannie tapped her toe. If he wasn't the most aggravating man alive. He was wrong, she was right and that was that. "As if I'd marry you on a bet anyway. You should be so lucky."

He made a rude sound.

"Okay, fine," she decided on the spur of the moment. "You're on."

Chapter Eight

Frannie and Drew managed to work together for an entire week without any major blowups. Which wasn't to say there hadn't been any close calls, Frannie admitted privately as she drove home Friday afternoon. Frannie had become very aware of her tongue and its placement in her mouth this past week. It would be difficult to discuss the *th* sound with her second-graders if the front of her tongue was missing. And quite frankly, she'd bitten back plenty of pithy responses to some of Drew's more inane observations on her work skills, personality, hair and everything else under the universe having to do with Frannie that he suddenly felt compelled to comment upon. It was pure luck her tongue was still whole. Somehow though, she suspected Drew had done the same, for there had been times—too few in Frannie's opinion—when she could tell he'd held back.

Truthfully, it made her kind of sad that things had reached the point where she and Drew couldn't be in the same room, heck, anywhere in the same vicinity, without there being tension. She mourned the loss of a good friend and was frustrated that it had been for naught. Drew was not interested in her, not as a woman.

How had it come to this?

"I wanted a lover and ended up losing a good friend," Frannie muttered as she reached over the seat for her insulated lunch tote. "Go figure." She slung the strap over her shoulder and started up the walk, muttering the whole way.

Opening the door, Frannie pulled her baseball cap off and threw it on the bench she kept by the door. She also dumped her purse, lunch box and keys and headed straight for the shower.

"Hot out there." She grabbed some clean underwear as she passed through her bedroom.

"Well, what do you want? It's the end of June." She took a towel from the tiny hall linen closet.

"Hope it doesn't rain this weekend." Frannie turned on the taps in the shower.

"Yeah, it would be bad to be cooped up inside with three little ones." She unhitched her shortalls and let them drop then stepped out of them.

"And that close to Drew for two and a half days straight?" Frannie shuddered and it wasn't from the water temperature she tested. "You'd probably end up killing him. Or he'd kill you, one or the other."

Frannie stepped into the tub and pulled the curtain. "I don't understand him. He's just so jumpy and irritable. Almost like he's scared. But of what? Listen to me, will you? I'm having a two-way conversation. With myself. Oh, my God." She bit her tongue, but gently, ever mindful of the consonant blends, diphthongs, etc. she'd be responsible for teaching during the coming school year.

An hour later, Frannie was finally ready. Overnighter in hand, she locked the front door again. Frannie had yet to say another word to herself. Sung along with the radio a few times, yes, spoken, no. Tossing the suitcase into the rear seat of her car, Frannie looked over the directions Drew had given her before driving to his sister's house. Typical of an engineer, Drew's instructions had been clear, precise and totally void of anything extraneous.

"Come on," she said, forgetting her vow of silence. "A few more landmarks so I'd know if I'd gone too far or not far enough wouldn't have killed you." Still, Frannie found his sister's place with no trouble. It just went to show how perverse she could be, Frannie supposed, but it almost would have been worth it to have gotten lost just so she could've complained about the lean, no-fat directions. It was six-thirty. "Drew took the afternoon off so Karen and her husband could be on their way," Frannie reminded herself as she hurried up the walk. "That means he's already been on his own for several hours. It's probably a disaster already in there."

She rang the bell and waited. And waited. Finally Frannie tried the knob. Locked.

"Okay," she breathed. "Now what? They couldn't all be dead already." She blew out a breath. "Although, the emergency room is a distinct possibility. Drew's not used to watching young children. All right, stay calm. Check the backyard first, then you can use the car phone to start calling hospitals."

Circling the house, she opened the gate to the yard. And thank God, there they were, sitting at a traditional wooden picnic table angled prettily on a brick patio attached to the back of the house. There was an open bucket of fried chicken, a bag of prewashed baby carrots and an open bag of chips spilling its contents next to a pitcher of brilliantly blue juice. None of the little faces were smiling as they picked listlessly at their food.

"Hey," Frannie said, snagging Drew's attention. He immediately rose and untangled his legs from the picnic bench to come to her.

"Hey, yourself," he greeted her. "I'll take that." He took her overnighter away from her so quickly Frannie thought he might be afraid of her escaping rather than performing an act of courtesy. Drew cocked a head towards the picnic bunch. "We've got a bunch of sourpusses over there," he said softly. "They're missing their mom and dad."

Frannie nodded wisely. "Ah."

"Yeah." He rocked on his heels, his hands in his shorts' pockets. "You, uh, eaten yet?"

Frannie shook her head. "No. Not yet."

"Yeah, well, no problem. I think I may have overbought. These guys don't seem to eat too much. There's plenty here for you and anyone else we may care to invite in off the streets."

Frannie grinned, but quickly put on a suitably sober mien before approaching the picnic table. Drew followed and performed the appropriate introductions.

"Frannie, this is my niece Chrissie, my nephew Daniel and my niece Samantha. Kids, say hello to my friend Frannie."

Frannie nodded at the glum bunch. "Hi, guys."

Chrissie, a brunette with lopsided pigtails and the oldest at about six or seven continued to torture the chicken leg on her plate with a fork as she studied Frannie with blue eyes too large for her little face. "Are you gonna stay over too? Like Uncle Drew?"

Frannie suddenly had the feeling she was in a minefield. "Well, yes, that was the plan. Is that okay with you?"

Daniel, the middle child and a full head shorter than Chrissie responded. "Mommy's gonna be mad."

"Yeah," Chrissie put in. "We're not allowed to have

friends over when there's a baby-sitter. Only when Mommy or Daddy is home. You're gonna get us all in trouble.''

"I talked to your mom before I invited Frannie, guys,'' Drew reassured them. "It's okay for her to be here, promise.'' But his quick reassurance only served to turn his pint-size crew against him.

"So how come you get to have friends over when they're not here and we can't? Huh? How come?''

Drew quickly threw up both hands in a peace gesture. "Hey, cool it, people. Frannie's not here to play with me like your friends are when they come over.''

Frannie tilted her head and looked at Drew out of the corner of her eyes. She'd like to play with him. Boy, would she. But it wasn't meant to be. She had to get over that and move on. That's what this weekend was for. The getting over and the moving on. Frannie told herself she probably wouldn't be able to stand Drew after spending close to sixty hours with him. The past week at work had made it obvious he already couldn't stand her. She hoped to be cured and be quite happily dating somebody else instead of feeling like she was settling in nothing flat.

"She's going to help me baby-sit all of you. There's three of you, remember and only one of me,'' Drew said as he loaded a paper plate with two large pieces of chicken, a ton of potato chips and about half a bag of baby carrots. He plopped it down at an empty spot and gestured for Frannie to sit. Evidently he felt she'd need to keep her strength up.

"Jeffie Monroe baby-sits us all by hisself. You could too,'' Daniel said. "If you wanted.''

Drew rolled his eyes. Six hours down and fifty-four to go. Dear God, be merciful. Zap me with a lightning bolt and take me now, Drew thought. "Jeffie Monroe is a lot younger than I am, Daniel,'' Drew declared. "I'm old and I'm going to need some help.'' He looked into each one of their eyes with what he hoped was a meaningful stare. "And I expect you guys to be nice to Frannie and to remember your manners."

Be firm, but in a nice way, and they'll be fine, his sister had said and Drew was trying, he really was. He just didn't think Karen knew her kids as well as she thought she did. Either that, or she'd neglected to explain to her kids that they were supposed to shape up when someone was nicely firm with them. Either way, this weekend was not going to be the piece of cake he'd been led to expect.

Frannie decided it was time to jump into the fray. She took a big bite of chicken, chewed and swallowed before casually saying, "It's all right if they're rude, Drew. I don't mind." She took another healthy chunk off the drumstick and smacked her lips enthusiastically. "Mmm, this is good." She waved the drumstick around to punctuate her words. "I mean, I really was in the mood for a game of kickball, but I bet there are kids down at the park who will play with me since these guys don't want me around.

"Probably I'll be hungry again when I'm done playing kickball, you know, all that exercise and everything. So, I figured I'd go to Thirty-One Flavors and get an ice cream cone. Maybe even a double scoop. Tin Roof Sundae and Rocky Road. Yeah, that sounds pretty good. Hope they have those two. Of course, if they don't I suppose I could always go to the grocery store. In fact that might be a good idea anyway. I could get some root beer and vanilla ice cream that way. I am sort of in the mood for a root beer float." Frannie shrugged. "By then I'll probably be tired so I thought I'd get ready for bed. Brush my teeth, put on my jammies, stuff like that. You know. I always like to read before I go to sleep. I have a new Harry Potter I've been wanting to start."

The kids' eyes were alternating between each other and Frannie. Their postures were nowhere near as slumped.

Chrissie had stopped torturing her food with her utensils and chomped down on a carrot instead as Frannie expanded on her list of activities.

"Do you like to read at night, Drew?"

Drew had noticed the glimmer of interest Frannie had managed to raise as well. "Why, yes I do. As a matter of fact, I kind of like to read out loud. And Harry Potter does sound good. Of course, I suppose since nobody's interested in doing anything tonight I could always just read quietly to myself."

Little Samantha, who was maybe two years old, finally piped up. "You could wead to me, Unca Dwew," she said. "I wike stowies."

"Thank you, Sam," said Drew. "That's nice of you to let me read to you. I appreciate it."

"I'll play kickball with you," Chrissie grudgingly offered. "It's better than just sitting here all bored and everything. I guess."

"And I like Bubble Gum ice cream," Daniel admitted. "In a sugar cone."

"Well, then, sounds like we have a plan," Frannie said with a smile. "But first things first. Uncle Drew and I can't buy ice cream for anybody who doesn't clean their plates or your mom will clobber us good, so eat up, people. Besides, you're all going to need lots of energy for kickball 'cuz I've got to tell you, I'm one good kicker and you just may be chasing that ball from here all the way out to the moon and back."

"Uncle Drew's lots bigger'n my mom. She could never clobber him. Heck, she hardly ever clobbers us. Only when we push her beyond...beyond..."

"Beyond human endurance," Chrissie helpfully supplied for her younger brother.

"Yeah, that," Daniel agreed. "Will you teach me how

to kick to the moon, Frannie?'' he asked. ''I want to be able to kick that far, too.''

''You need lots of strength to kick to the moon,'' Frannie advised. ''So the first thing we've got to do is eat up all our baby carrots and chicken meat, okay?''

Daniel nodded agreeably and crunched down on a carrot. Not willing to be left out, Chrissie quickly followed suit. Without making a production out of it, Frannie slid down next to the littlest one and cut her food into manageable pieces. Samantha, quickly picking up on the rise in the sibling mood barometer, popped the pieces into her mouth and happily ate as quickly as Frannie produced them.

Drew shot her a look of gratitude and relief from across the table. ''Thank you,'' he mouthed.

Frannie nodded. ''My pleasure,'' she mouthed back and meant it.

After a quick post-dinner cleanup involving not much more than tossing out the used paper products and stowing the leftovers in the fridge, the group ambled down to the park. Chrissie had a large, semi-soft ball under one arm and Daniel hugged another to his chest. ''In case we lose one when we kick it into outer space,'' he explained. ''Or if one of the big boys at the park takes it and runs away with it. That happened to Billy Jackson once when me and him was playing whiffle ball.''

Quite frankly, Frannie considered the second possibility more likely than the first although she certainly wasn't about to say as much. ''I know what you mean,'' she said instead. ''I had some big boys take away my jump rope and hide it just to be mean when I was not much older than you.''

Daniel's eyes widened as he discovered a soul mate. ''What did you do?'' he asked.

''I cried,'' Frannie admitted matter of factly. ''How about you?''

"Me too!" Daniel said in amazement.

"But then your Uncle Drew made them give it back. He was my hero that day."

Daniel gazed at the uncle in question. "Really?"

"Uh-huh. Really," Frannie said.

"Weren't you scared, Uncle Drew?"

"Yeah, but I was more mad."

"Wow." Daniel appeared thoughtful for a moment. "Uncle Drew?"

"Yeah, champ?"

"If the big boys bother us, will you make them go away?"

"I'll kick their sorry butts all the way to the moon. Then they can pick up all the balls Frannie's kicked that far and worry about how to get them home."

"You will?"

"You bet."

Daniel digested that. "Wow."

Frannie stifled a grin and dropped back a couple of paces so she could walk beside Drew. She took his hand and squeezed. "You're his hero now," she said quietly.

"Some things never change, do they?" he asked just as quietly.

"I guess not."

"Well, nobody's going to pick on these kids while I'm around."

Squeezing his hand once more, Frannie responded, "No. They're not." And unfortunately, she loved him even more for his protectiveness. Darn, she sure hoped this weekend didn't turn out to be a bust in terms of getting over Drew.

"I was really counting on this."

"Hmm?"

"What? Oh, nothing," Frannie said, dropping his hand like a live coal when she realized she had it clutched in hers. "Nothing," she reiterated more for herself.

Chrissie knew a couple of kids at the park. A boy and a girl. Twins, she said, in her class at school. Another smaller boy that Daniel "sort of" knew was there along with a friend of his. They were all quickly recruited with Frannie taking charge of one group of midgets and Drew squiring the other. It wasn't long before the "big kids" who were all of maybe eight or nine realized they were being left out of the fun and wanted to join as well.

Several of them swaggered over and one announced, "Jake and Buddy and me will play on the same side as him." He pointed to Drew. "And I'll be the pitcher."

Drew balanced the kickball on his fingertips as he contemplated the young man in front of him. "What's your name?"

"Joe."

"Well, Joe, if you play at all, and that will be Chrissie and Daniel's decision, you'll all split up so the teams will be fair. The teams already have pitchers, but we'll probably rotate, so it's possible you may have a turn at pitching, but maybe not. A lot will depend on attitude." Drew flipped the ball. It arched up into the air. He caught it in his other hand. "You still want to play?"

Joe flipped his overly long bangs out of his eyes with a toss of his head. He slouched and shifted his weight from one cocked hip to the other. He glanced at his buddies and found little support there. They were eyeing the youngster practicing kicking, their bodies eagerly shadowing her movements. "Yeah, I guess," he finally allowed ungraciously.

Drew raised a brow in Chrissie's direction. "Chrissie?" he said, inquiringly.

She hesitated long enough to let Drew know she wasn't thrilled before nodding. He turned to Daniel. "Danny boy?"

Daniel looked from the eight-year-olds to his uncle and

back. Drew could practically see his mind work. Three against one, but still his uncle was way bigger. "You remember what you said, Uncle Drew?" the boy asked uneasily.

"I remember," Drew said firmly and flexed his biceps, showing Daniel the muscle he made. "Let's see yours." He nodded at the pathetic muscle the four-year-old made. "Looks like we've got them covered, kiddo."

Daniel laughed. "Okay, then. If they be bad, they're gonna have a long walk home."

"That's right," Drew said with a nod. "All the way from the moon, Danny boy." Drew pointed to the sky. "From the moon."

"We get Jake and Buddy 'cuz we were one short. Chrissie's side can have Joe."

"Good idea," Drew approved. "That will even off the teams."

Daniel glowed with the compliment and Frannie suspected Drew had won a fan for life. She watched as Drew rubbed his hands together. "All right, people, time to play ball. Batter, er, I mean, kicker up!"

Once Joe realized that the game was where the fun was and he was not going to be allowed to bully anyone, he dropped the act and got into the spirit of things. Before long, both teams had filled out. Even a few parents joined in, which kept the side-line heckling good-spirited and ensured the little ones got their fair turns.

"All right, Samantha, you're up," Frannie called from the pitcher's spot.

"Keep your eye on the ball, Sammie," Drew called. "Here it comes."

The two-year-old was primed as she watched the ball gently roll towards her. She was shaking she was so primed, one leg supporting her chubby little body while the other was back, ready to take off. Her fists were clenched and her arms ready to pump.

"Now, Samantha, now," Frannie yelled as the ball all but stopped in front of the tyke. "Go! Run! Kick it!"

The little one gave it her all. She ran at the ball, drew her leg back, but instead of giving the ball a good swift kick, her foot skimmed over the top. Samantha lost her balance and sat on the ball which skidded out from under her, dumping the little one flat on her back. Samantha promptly began to wail.

"Ow! Ow! Ow! It huwts! It huwts!"

Frannie raced in from what passed as the mound while Drew hotfooted it in from the sidelines. They met over Samantha's sobbing writhing body.

"What hurts, baby girl?"

"Shhh, sweetheart. Shhh. Let us see now. Where's the owie?"

"Did you hit your head? Frannie, what if she has a concussion? Should we call an ambulance?"

Samantha held her arms up to Frannie. "I sitted down too hawd. I huwted my bottom, Fwannie. Maybe it's even bwoked."

"Okay, sugar, okay." Frannie leaned into the girl's open arms allowing Samantha to wrap her arms around her without moving her. "I need you to lie still now while Uncle Drew and I check things out."

By now Samantha was surrounded by children of varying ages. The adults were also crowding close.

"Hey, Frannie?" Daniel questioned, his voice wavering.

Frannie was running her hands over Samantha's plump little legs and arms, checking for any further damage other than a broken bottom. "What is it, honey?"

"When Chrissie broked her arm they put a cast on it. Mommy said it was to hold the bones still so they could fix themselves. I got to write my name on it and draw a

TERRY ESSIG 139

picture of Chrissie walking on top of the fence in the backyard like the tightrope walker at the circus. Only *she* didn't
fall off like Chrissie did.''

"Yeah? I'm sure she loved the picture, Daniel.''

"So I was just thinking, if Sammie broked her bottom
and they put a cast on it, how's she goin' to go potty?''

Drew and Frannie exchanged a look.

"Ah, well—''

"Chwissie had her cast on foweveh!'' Samantha
shrieked. "Didn't you, Chwissie? I gotta go potty now! I
can't hold it foweveh!'' And little Samantha promptly
grabbed her crotch and held on for dear life.

"Shhh, sweetheart. I don't think you broke your bottom,
honestly, I don't. Shh, shh. Take a deep breath now.''

"Don't worry, Sammie. My cast had lots of cool drawings on it. Everybody signed their names and everything.''

"No! I don't want a cast on my bottom and it's bwoked,
I know it is. It's bwoked foh sure! I can never go potty
again!''

"No, no, sweetie. I think you just bruised it a little bit.
Come on now, stop crying and let me check you over.''

Daniel interrupted. "But what if—''

"Drew,'' Frannie ruthlessly interrupted, "Why don't you
get Daniel and Chrissie to help you keep everyone back?
Sammie could use a little breathing space, don't you
think?''

"What? Oh, oh, sure. No problem. Come on, Daniel,
Chrissie.''

"But Uncle Drew—''

"For crying out loud, Daniel, I'm an engineer. If she
broke her bottom, you and I will design a system for her
so she can go potty. Now quit your worrying.''

"Really?''

"You bet. Drainage fields are my specialty, after all. A

little more volume than we're talking here, but what the hey.''

''Cool. We got some old garden hose at home. Maybe if we—''

''Uh-huh, uh-huh. Sounds good, kid. Let's head over this way and we'll talk. Come on, Chrissie, you too.''

Frannie shook her head at the departing trio, but was in no position to criticize. Drew was successfully removing Daniel from the scene and keeping him distracted at the same time. She could hardly wait to see the design for their drainage system. It would probably work. As another parent began shepherding kids back, Frannie knelt back down beside Samantha and leaned down.

''Samantha? I want you to listen to me, all right? Wiggle your toes for me, sweetie. That's it. Now I want you to try and bend your knee. Can you do that? Very good.''

Deprived of her audience and faced with Frannie's matter-of-fact demeanor, Samantha rapidly calmed down. As Frannie worked her way up Samantha's body, asking her to move various parts, it soon became evident she'd done no serious damage. There was absolutely no sign of spinal injury or concussion.

Soon the little girl was back on her feet and Frannie was helping to dust off her bottom.

''There you go, Sammie. Good as new.''

''No. My shohts is dirty.'' Samantha twisted her body in an attempt to see behind herself. She pointed to a mud smear on her backside. ''Look,'' she commanded. ''See?''

''We'll wash them,'' Frannie assured her.

Samantha's lower lip still stuck out a good half inch. ''I still don't want to play no moah.''

Frannie debated the wisdom of making the two-year-old get right back up to try and kick the ball again. Weren't you supposed to face your fears right away so they didn't cripple you later in life? You know, jump right back in the water when you almost drown otherwise you'll be afraid of the water for the rest of your life?

Chewing her lip for all of a second and a half, Frannie decided to heck with it. Her goal was to help Drew keep the three children he was in charge of alive for the weekend. Their parents could deal with the psychological damage done in the process. She was not going to knowingly send a two-year-old into a temper tantrum by trying to make her do something that was not essential for the salvation of her soul or the preservation of her life.

Wasn't that age group renowned for their screaming fits?

Why, yes, they were. Frannie answered her own question.

Wasn't that why they were called the terrible twos, after all?

Why yes, it was.

This was a no-brainer.

"It's okay, sweetie. You don't have to kick the ball any more. It's getting late anyway." She smiled down at Samantha. "You know what I think? I think we should all go get some ice cream."

Samantha's lower lip retracted like magic and she began to jump up and down. "Yay! Ice cweam! Ice cweam! I love ice cweam."

A two-year-old that loved ice cream. Who'd have guessed?

Chrissie, who'd sneaked away from Drew to rejoin Frannie, threw up her hands and yelled, "Our side wins 'cuz your side quit. We win!"

"Nooo," Samantha immediately protested. "We winned. We twied weally hadd and I almost bwoked my bottom so my team wins!"

"Yeah, but you quit so—"

Man, they'd been so close, Frannie thought as she rolled her eyes. One crisis almost averted and here came another

one. How did parents do this twenty-four-seven? She was
writing her mom and dad a thank-you note as soon as this
weekend was over. The mere fact that she and her brothers
were still alive was tribute to her parents' fortitude. They'd
raised them all without losing a one of them to an accident
or premeditated murder. A card might not be enough. Flowers too?

Back to the battleground for now. She'd think about an
appropriate token of appreciation later. "Chrissie, are you
sure you want to do this? We can't take arguing children
into the ice cream place, now can we? If you two start
fighting, we'll have to go straight home instead of going
out for a treat. How about if we call it a tie? Both sides
did have the same number of runs, after all."

It was a tough decision to make and ended up taking a
good ten or more seconds. Even then, it was reluctantly
given. "Well, okay, I guess." Then Chrissie said in a quiet
rush, "But really we won."

Drew, noticing the dispersing crowd, rejoined the group.
"Okay, people, Danny boy and I have it just about figured
out. If anybody really does break their bottom," and here
he winked at Frannie, "Dan and I know how to handle it.
The trick is to take a length of garden hose with you to the
hospital. Then, before they put the cast on you ask them to
duct tape the hose down one leg and—"

Frannie didn't want to hear it. She really didn't. Not
when she was about to eat dessert. She reached up and put
a hand over Drew's mouth. "Not now, Drew." Maybe not
later either.

"Mmmph."

It was going to be a long weekend.

Drew stuck out his tongue and swiped the palm of Frannie's hand with it. She jumped and her blood pressure
spiked. He grinned at her.

A very long weekend.

Chapter Nine

It took "foheveh" to walk to the ice cream parlor from the park. It took "foheveh" to get served. And it took forever times two, no, make that forever squared, to clean up the filthy, sticky, grass-stained threesome.

Frannie gently tugged the last snarl free from Samantha's freshly shampooed head. "There. All done. Go pick out a story. Uncle Drew's waiting to read it to you."

Drew, who'd been collapsed on one side of his sister's king-size bed, flat on his back with hands folded across his chest like a corpse ready for viewing, while Frannie sat on its end patiently desnarling Samantha's hair, cocked open one closed eye. "I am?"

"You are," Frannie affirmed as Samantha scampered out of the master bedroom in hot pursuit of her favorite reading material. Frannie made it to the other side of the large bed before collapsing herself. "They're your nieces and nephews, after all. And I took care of both girls. All you had to do was get one little boy ready for bed. I did twice the work. Don't think I didn't notice."

"I should have known you'd be keeping some kind of score card," Drew sighed.

"Damn straight. I didn't grow up with a bunch of take-advantage older brothers for nothing."

"Yeah, whatever. And I wasn't taking advantage. I just didn't think it would look right for a guy to be bathing little girls, that's all," Drew declared with seeming altruism.

Frannie snorted. She wasn't buying any of it. "Yeah, right. Your sister's ten kinds of a fool if she lets your brother-in-law get away with anything like that."

Drew opened both eyes, sat up and propped a pillow behind his head. There was nothing quite as invigorating as one of the ridiculous arguments he and Frannie so easily got into. "He's their father, which is different and if my sister wanted more help in that department, she should have had all boys."

"Okay, Mr. College Graduate. It's the man who decides the sex, but don't let facts get in your way."

"That's a vicious rumor started by one of Henry the Eighth's wives when she couldn't produce a son," Drew virtuously maintained.

That got a rise out of Frannie. She found the strength to sit back up and poke Drew in the chest. "Oh, right. I get it now."

Drew recoiled. "Hey, watch out. Get a manicure, will you? Man, you got lethal weapons there, Frannie." He rubbed his chest where she'd poked him.

Rolling her eyes, Frannie poked him again. "Don't be such a baby. I barely touched you. And furthermore, your brother-in-law—what's his name?"

"Chuck." He kept a cautious eye on the freewheeling finger.

"Well I think good old Chuck probably purposely pro-duced girls just to get out of the bathing routine. If that isn't just like a man. Anything to get out of a little work.

He figured out some kind of Y chromosome inhibitor. That's what I think.''

Drew made a grab for the finger before it could jab him again. "Trust me, he's not that smart. You'll have to meet him sometime, see what I mean.''

"Oh, yeah? Then why'd your sister marry him?'' Frannie struggled to free her finger, but Drew wasn't letting go. In fact, she was being inexorably pulled towards Drew. Darn, he was strong.

"Like I said, you'll have to get to know him. Chuck doesn't smoke and isn't very polite to people who do. His paycheck is direct-deposited with no surcharges paid at the corner bar or the race track. I think I've heard him swear maybe twice in my life. He's steady, reliable and he was crazy about Karen. Not being a fool, she snapped him right up.''

Frannie made a rude sound. "Oh, please.'' Guys like that didn't exist. Although, Drew didn't smoke, drink or gamble. He was reliable, too. Too bad he didn't have the sense to worship at Frannie's feet.

"Hey, you don't even know him, Frannie. He's a genuinely nice guy. How can you accuse him of shirking without even meeting him? He and Karen just need some time alone. They'll be fine, I was just in a bad mood the other night.'' She was sure pretty when she got all riled up. Needling her was a sheer pleasure.

"He's a man, isn't he?'' Frannie asked rhetorically. "That says it all as far as I'm concerned. It'll take more than a weekend to overcome a handicap like that.'' Her finger was still trapped.

Drew gave one final tug and Frannie ended up sprawled across his lap. He looked down at her. "Know what I think? I think you're jealous.''

"That's ridiculous. Of what?''

"I think you're jealous because Karen is living the

American dream. Well, the female version, anyway, and you're not. You've yet to find the guy who'll take one look at you and lose his good sense.'' Although a thorough study of her snapping brown eyes and prettily flushed complexion had him wondering about that.

Nonplused with both her position and Drew's proximity, Frannie sputtered. ''Oh, yeah? Well any day now Paul or Brian is going to ask me out. Just wait and see.''

Drew's expression immediately darkened. ''You watch yourself with those two,'' he ordered.

Frannie stared up the short distance to his face, struck as always by the intense blueness of his eyes. ''I thought you said all your people were good guys. Out to save the world and all of that.''

''And I don't want to be proved wrong, either.'' Not when it was Frannie who would suffer. Just look at her, lying across his lap all soft, sun-kissed and right-looking. Mostly right-looking, Drew realized. He couldn't help it. ''You are so damn cute,'' he announced and then Drew kissed her.

Frannie was stunned when Drew's lips first connected with hers. He was not a touchy-feely kind of guy. At least, not with her. And the few times Frannie had kissed him, Drew had acted all flustered. So what was this? Then the kiss became more involved with Drew gently kneading her scalp and slipping his tongue into her surprised mouth to play. Once that happened, well, who the heck could care about the what and why?

It would take a better person than Frannie to worry about all that, for sure. She was content to simply enjoy.

''Um, you taste like peppermint. And chocolate,'' she confided.

''And what was it you had, Rocky Road?'' Drew softly inquired. ''Pretty damn good.'' And it was. He drew her up closer, held her tighter as he went back for a second taste. It was even better. He let his tongue swirl around hers. It only took one arm to prop her up, she was so light, which left the other hand free to roam.

And he let it.

Down her ribs to the hem of her T-shirt then sliding up underneath the fabric, craving the touch of her soft skin. Again he indulged himself, lightly rubbing her smooth torso. His fingers tingled by the time he'd found the bottom of her bra. It was a little nothing of a bra, the fabric thin and as silky as her skin. He hated it anyway and pushed it up, out of his way.

Frannie needed something to hang on to as her world tilted and sensation after sensation washed over her. She looped an arm up over his shoulder and behind his neck and hung on for dear life. "Drew?" she whispered against his mouth, unsure of what was happening to her.

Drew pulled his mouth back a centimeter or two. No more than two. "Darn it all, you feel good," he muttered before gently locking back on. Their teeth lightly clinked together and he backed off, but not much. He wanted to inhale her, but that would mean losing contact with the breast he held in the palm of his hand. Drew wasn't about to let that happen. Not when it felt so right exactly where it was.

You know, for an engineer graduated from Purdue, one of the top engineering schools in the country, Drew was beginning to feel kind of stupid. How could he have not known how perfectly Frannie's breast would fit into his hand? Not too big, not too small, but just right. Hell, a kid reading the fairy tale "Goldilocks and the Three Bears" would have been able to figure it out. Structurally—

Ah, how could he think about structure when her hard little nipples were poking him? One prodded his chest while the other nudged his hand. He separated his second and third fingers, letting her nipple slide into the opening he

created, then lightly compressed. Frannie moaned and restlessly shifted. Drew couldn't help but wonder if he could
make her come by caressing her breasts alone. She seemed
that responsive.

Scientists were ever interested in experimenting, so he
quite literally bent himself to the task and hoped to high
heaven *he* could last long enough to see it through. He
smoothed her shirt up and planted a kiss on her abdomen.
He nuzzled the underside of one breast.

"I found it, Unca Dwew! I finally founded it!" Samantha
hurtled her little body through the doorway and flung herself on the bed. She was closely followed by Daniel and
Chrissie.

"I hate that one, Uncle Drew. She *always* picks the same
one and it's dumb. Read mine instead." Daniel jumped on
the bed and thrust a book into Drew's face.

"No, no. Don't read theirs, Uncle Drew. They're *both*
dumb. Here. This one's really good. It's got chapters and
everything." One more body landed on the bed with aban-
don.

Drew almost bit off his own tongue, he removed his
mouth from Frannie's chest and snapped it shut so quickly.
Frannie, meanwhile simply could not believe they'd forgotten there were impressionable children in the house.
Hell's bells, it was the children's house, after all, and she
moved quickly to pull her T-shirt back down, then reached
underneath in an attempt to discreetly wrestle her bra back
into place. Holy mackerel. What had gotten into her?

"My book! My book!"

"It's dumb!"

"Is not. You's dumb."

"What were you guys doin'?"

So much for discreet.

Frannie issued the standard disclaimer. "Nothing."

Yeah, right. If they went for that, they were dumber than bricks.

"Why was you kissin' Fwannie's tummy? Does she got an owie?"

See? They were young, not stupid. "Uh—"

"Yeah, but I kissed it better," Drew said.

"He was practicing his raspberries," Frannie said simultaneously.

They looked at each other. "Um—"

All three children looked at them in confusion.

"It didn't make any sound," Daniel pointed out.

"Yeah," piped in Samantha. "Wazbewwies is supposed to make noise. *Lots* of noise," she stressed and putting mouth to arm demonstrated a properly blown raspberry.

"How did you hurt your tummy?" Chrissie wanted to know, having picked up on Drew's explanation rather than Frannie's. "Can I see it? We're not supposed to hold sticks on the playground at school. But Hannah Lindahl did it anyway? And she tripped and got it stuck in her leg. Right here." Chrissie pointed to a spot on her thigh. "Mrs. Richie said it she was lucky 'cuz it coulda been her *eye*—how come teachers and moms always think you're gonna poke out your eye? And she wouldn't let her take it out, neither. She said it would bleed like stink if the stick got pulled out and that only the doctor should take it out. But you know what? It bled like stink anyway. It was really gross," Chrissie reported with relish. "Is *your* tummy bleeding, Frannie? I don't 'member you holding a stick at the playground."

"Uh, no, it's not and no I wasn't. It was a stomachache," Frannie decided on the spot. "No blood involved. First your Uncle Drew kissed it better. It was just a small ache, you know. Then, once it was all better, he was just starting to practice his raspberries when you all came in." Not a half-bad story, Frannie decided proudly. Not bad at all.

"Well, he should practice some more," Daniel maintained. "Because there wasn't any noise. None at all."

"You're right," Frannie said and watched Drew raise an eyebrow. "But you know what I think?"

They all shook their heads in the negative, Drew especially vigorously, which didn't surprise Frannie. He'd never really had a clue where she was concerned.

"I think it might be possible that maybe Uncle Drew's raspberries are just fine and it's my stomach that has the problem. What do you think? Any of you guys willing to volunteer and see if they work on your tummies?"

Obviously the same genetic code ran through them all as all three quickly pulled up their pj tops and offered their tummies in the name of science. Drew tested them all. Wonder of wonders, he got a sufficiently loud sound and enough giggles from the recipients to satisfy everyone. Crisis averted. Or so Frannie thought. It was time to read the stories and the mood in the room quickly degenerated. Drew finally read both Samantha's and Daniel's both along with a chapter from Chrissie's. It was after ten o'clock before they were all settled into bed.

"Maybe they'll sleep later in the morning," Frannie said, exhausted.

"Maybe," Drew said, not sounding particularly convincing. "It's a nice thought." He sighed. "But probably they'll just be crabby from not getting enough sleep."

"We'll have them take a nap," Frannie instantly decided. "Or at the very least, a quiet time after lunch."

Drew liked the idea. "Good plan."

They sat there, slumped on opposite ends of the family-room sofa while low-volume music swirled around them, soothing their frazzled nerves. Drew had put it on. Frannie had been unable to watch television or use any kind of sound system anywhere but her own home—which she kept simple and to a bare minimum of remotes and crisscrossing wires, since the invention of cable. Digital really had her flummoxed. She cheerfully admitted to being totally technologically challenged but was very grateful tonight for Drew's engineer's brain. Frannie rested her head back against the sofa and closed her eyes, letting the soothing old melodies seep into her bones. They really knew how to croon back in the forties. "Good music," she finally murmured.

"Mmm." He sounded half asleep. "Frannie?"

"Hmm?"

"This is going to sound stupid."

"What?"

"I had a good time tonight."

She turned her head in his direction, her surprise tempered by exhaustion. "Yeah?"

"Yeah. This is hard for me to say, but here's the thing. I couldn't have done it without you. I'd have had to shoot myself. Or them. One or the other. I don't know, though, with you, it was frustrating and tiring but I still had fun. I, uh, just wanted you to know that."

"Thanks, Drew."

"You're welcome."

An old Frank Sinatra started up. The sound stole into the room and wrapped around Frannie, making her feel all warm and golden. An unbidden smile crept across her mouth and her upper body swayed in place a little bit, keeping time.

"Hey, Drew?"

"Hmm?"

"Recognize this?"

Drew listened for a moment, trying to concentrate, but his brain had punched out about an hour before. Finally he said, "Isn't this the song from Evie and Rick's wedding? That first dance thing?"

Frannie continued to smile to herself. "Yeah. I'm pretty sure it is."

"Nice," he offered.

"Yeah."

Drew cleared his throat. "You know, their wedding wasn't so bad, I guess. I mean, if you have to get married. But when I tie the knot? I'm not doing that feed-the-cake-to-each-other thing. Or the garter thing. Nobody's seeing that far up my woman's leg but me."

Frannie's eyes popped open. He'd said when. Not if, when.

"Other than that, it wasn't too bad. I guess those tuxedo shirts and the green cummerbunds weren't too stupid or anything. Frannie?"

"Yes?"

"Rick said Evie always dreamed about having a horse-drawn carriage with white horses take her and whoever she married from the church to the reception."

"Goes back to the Cinderella thing, I think," Frannie said smiling as she remembered how radiant Evie had been as her brother had helped her up into the coach.

"I guess." Quiet. Then, "You have anything special you've always wanted for your wedding day?"

Her eyes popped open again. "Sure."

"What?"

"Drew, I was a little girl. It was silly."

"Tell me."

She sighed. Okay, what was the harm? It wasn't like any of it could come true. "Oh, all right. Here goes." Frannie shoved a hand back through her hair, a bit embarrassed by what she was about to confess. "It was a summer Olympic year and I was little when I first got the idea. That's all I remember. Anyway, synchronized swimming was on. I'm not sure it was even an event, it may have only been an exhibition, that's how long ago this was."

Drew grunted. "Quit issuing disclaimers and get it out. You watched a synchronized swimming event." Although what that could have to do with weddings, he had no idea. But he could hardly wait to hear. He'd long ago accepted the fact that Frannie's brain was wired a little differently. "Go on."

"So, I made some remark to Mom about how pretty I thought it was and how could they hold their breath so long?"

"Yeah, okay. I'm still with you." He just wasn't sure exactly where that was.

"Next thing I knew she'd found some old Esther Williams movies at a video place that specialized in oldies. You ever see one of those?" Frannie asked, smiling softly as she remembered the wonder of that time so long ago.

"No, but my guess is this is someone who swam in movies."

"Got it in one. Her movies are back from the time when Hollywood was making spectaculars. You know, all these scantily clad girls with head pieces as tall as they were, all tap dancing down a staircase in absolute unison to be greeted at the bottom by a stage full of guys in top hats and tails, holding walking sticks." Just thinking about it had it all coming back.

"My Mom made me sit through *Funny Girl* with Barbra Streisand one night. When she was feeling lonely after Dad left. I remember there were a couple of scenes like that. You want a Ziegfeld Follies kind of wedding?" And he'd thought the idea of green wedding outfits had been horrifying. This was beyond horrifying. This went right off the horrifying scale and into the stratosphere. Drew couldn't think of a single guy of his acquaintance who would learn to tap dance for his wedding, regardless of the number of points and turns on top it earned him. Certainly not him. What red-blooded, real male would?

Frannie ignored him. This was her fantasy, after all and he'd asked. "There I was, my Ken and Barbie dolls on my lap, when suddenly it came to me."

Drew closed his eyes and groaned. "What?"

"Well, actually I'm not too sure," she said.

"What a surprise," Drew muttered under his breath.

"I mean, there are a couple of really cool possibilities here."

Not that he'd noticed. And did he really want to know? "Such as?" He couldn't help himself. He must be a glutton for punishment.

"Such as, oh I don't know, saying vows on a high diving board. Then, at the end of the ceremony, my groom and I would dive down into the center of a circle of synchronized swimmers all doing funky things with their legs. You should see some of the overhead shots of that kind of thing in the old movies. So cool."

"You'd drown," Drew predicted darkly. "Not only would your dress be ruined but when all that fabric got wet it would pull you straight down to the bottom of the pool. And your fancy hairdo it took all that time to do up for Rick's wedding would get wrecked as well. The hairdresser lady would kill you." And the final blow? "Besides, your makeup would run all over your face. You'd hate that." Every woman he'd ever known was constantly checking their makeup. She'd never do it, not for real. Please, God. The prayer was a real plea as the more time he spent with Frannie the more he was realizing that not only was she all grown up, but she was a special kind of woman with *permanence* stamped all over. He was starting to develop a sick feeling in the bottom of his stomach. Probably dread, because crossed brain wires and all, Mary Frances Parker just might have a permanent place in his future. The word *inevitable* was starting to resonate in his head. Actually, darkly toll was more like it.

"I didn't say it wouldn't require some special consid- erations," Frannie said, unaware of Drew's inner turmoil and beginning to get irritated. "And besides, mascara doesn't run in fantasies. It stays where it's supposed to. And you can buy waterproof. No, the big problem that I see is how do I get the guests up high enough to get the overhead view? I mean, that's the best part, after all. You'd have to have stadium seating or something."

"Marry an engineer," Drew advised, desperately fight- ing getting drawn into the problem. "Let him worry about that part. Like I said, you'll have your hands full keeping yourself from drowning."

Frannie flicked his concern away. "Piece of cake."

"Waterproof, I hope," Drew shot back. "Especially if they're going to be floating it out to you in the middle of the pool."

"Ew, soggy wedding cake. That's certainly a revolting mental picture."

Like the rest of what she'd confessed wasn't?

"And I wouldn't drown. I'd have this cool white se- quinned swimsuit with a long shimmery wrap-around skirt held on with Velcro, maybe." She gave it some consider- ation. "Yeah, Velcro would work. Right before we dove in I'd whip it off and fling it into the crowd. And the veil would be attached to one of those old-time bathing caps. The ones with fake flowers all over it? Or wait, my grand- mother had one with fake hair on the outside, like a wig. You know, I never understood why, if the purpose of a bathing cap is to keep hair out of the filter, then why did they make caps with hair on the outside of them?" She shrugged. "Anyway, the bathing cap will keep my real hair nice and dry so that when we get to the reception part, it'll still look good."

Could the woman not see how nuts this was? It was demoralizing that he was as attracted to her as he was.

"Instead of a veil, why don't you wear a regular bathing cap with one of those big white floppy hats with ribbons and gunk all over it on top of it so nobody sees it? Then, when you whip off your skirt for the grand finale, you can whip the hat off as well,'' Drew facetiously suggested.

Frannie's eyes lit up. "Great idea."

Only Frannie would take a suggestion like that seriously. "You're nuts, you know that? Heck, why not have the guests on the shore of a lake and when it's time, you get pulled in on a barge which then gets anchored in front of them for the ceremony? When it's all over and time to leave on the honeymoon, jump into a canoe and just paddle away. That way, in case your prospective groom has a fear of heights,'' which it just so happened Drew did, "he won't be quite so terrified during the ceremony." Although anybody marrying Frannie ought to be anyway.

Frannie thought about it. "It has possibilities," she decided.

Drew snorted. "I was kidding."

Another slow Sinatra number came on. "Frannie?"

"Hmm?"

"You want to dance?" He wanted her in his arms and there was also the slim possibility that dancing might actually shut her up.

Being a sad case and still jumping at any chance to be held by Drew, Frannie said yes.

Drew moved them slowly, dreamily around the living room, adeptly avoiding the coffee table, sofa and side chairs. "I never thought I'd say so, but I'm glad your mother talked mine into making us all take dance lessons that summer."

"Yes. It was fun."

Drew snorted. "It was torture." He tugged lightly, pulling Frannie in closer against his body. "But worth it. Now."

She'd died and gone to heaven, Frannie thought as she snuggled against Drew's chest. Their old dance instructor, Ms. Timmler, would have heart failure if she could see their dance posture. No way should they be this close. No way should Drew drop her right hand from his and pull her arm up around his neck so that both her arms looped around his neck. Uh-oh, Drew was rubbing his stubble-roughened cheek against her hair, snagging it, turning his face to put his nose into it. Oh yeah, Ms. Timmler would have smacked him upside the head for sure. Good thing she wasn't here, Frannie thought muzzily because while it may not be how to do the dance, etiquettically speaking, she sure didn't want him to stop.

That old bat who'd taught them how to dance, Ms. What-ever-her-name-was, would never recognize Drew's version of the foxtrot, Drew decided, snugging Frannie in even closer, one hand riding low on her spine, the other boldly splaying across her rear as he held her hips firmly against his own. She felt good, as though she belonged there in his arms, her hair tickling his nose and smelling of something flowery.

At the end of the song, Drew reluctantly backed off. The dance had effectively shut Frannie up. She was cuddled up like a contented cat against his chest. The problem wasn't Frannie. The problem was himself, Drew admitted wryly. His sex was rising to the occasion, so to speak, and a house full of young children was not going to provide the opportunity to alleviate the problem. Anyway, Frannie was worth more than a quick roll in the hay. He gritted his teeth. This just might kill him, but it was probably best to call it a night.

"What's the matter?" Frannie murmured when Drew carefully set her aside. She swayed for a moment before she caught her balance, feeling the loss of Drew's support.

"Nothing," Drew said, his chest and arms cool without

Frannie's warmth. "I just figured the kids'll be getting up early. We should try to get some sleep." He fought the urge to reach down and adjust his zipper. If Frannie didn't realize there was a problem he wasn't about to point it out. Right about now, his poor sex probably didn't know up from down. It had spent the time since Frannie's arrival at suppertime in a state of confusion, not knowing if it should be up, down or somewhere in between. It had tried them all. Several times. Man, if exercise built you up, the guys in his health club's locker room were in for some serious competition. Not that they didn't get it anyway, of course.

"Oh," said Frannie, blinking stupidly. "Okay. You're right. We should probably go to bed." But she didn't want to. At least not without Drew. Reluctantly, Drew's hand guiding her from the small of her back, they started down the hallway to the bedrooms.

"You take Karen and Chuck's bed. I'll sleep out here on the sofa. Let me just grab one of the pillows off the bed and a sheet from the linen closet," Drew said.

"That's silly," Frannie protested. "The sofa's not big enough for you. I'll sleep out here, you take the bed."

"Frannie, just once could you not argue?"

"I'm not arguing, I just—oh, wait. I forgot to tell you something."

A feeling of foreboding swept over Drew. Frannie's memory lapses were usually highly selective. He just knew he wasn't going to like this. "What?"

"Nothing much. You're going to be on your own for an hour or two in the morning, that's all."

"On my own! What? You can't be serious. Where are you going? You'll have to take at least two of them with you." He loved his nieces and nephew dearly, but en masse they scared the pants off him. Especially when he was in charge of their physical safety and mental well-being.

"I won't be gone all that long," Frannie soothed. "I

have a dental appointment. I'm getting my teeth cleaned, that's all. Couple of hours, tops."

"You just had your teeth cleaned over spring break. I know. Your car was in the shop. I drove you."

"Yes, well, um…"

"Wait just a minute here. I get it now. Your appointment isn't with Dr. Chandler, is it?"

"Uh…"

"I knew it! It's with that other guy, isn't it? The one up on the billboard with the nostrils big enough to drive a fire truck up."

"Now, Drew, proportionately, his nostrils are just fine. I mean, his whole face has been blown up to the size of a billboard, after all."

"I can't believe you're doing this! I thought if I gave you a summer job, you'd be safe. You'd quit all this nonsense."

"The *purpose* of getting summer job was to help find me a spouse, remember? Since I'm not working for him, I thought I could still check him out by…letting him clean my teeth." Frannie shrugged. It had seemed a good idea at the time.

Drew backed her up against the hall wall, caging her in with his arms on either side of her head. "Like a horse getting his teeth checked before being purchased?"

"Well, I—"

"You're not going."

"Yes, I am."

"Then we're all coming with you."

"Be reasonable, Drew. It takes forty-five minutes to an hour to get your teeth cleaned. Are you really going to sit in the waiting room that long with three kids crawling all over you, tearing the place apart?" Drew sounded almost…jealous. Could it be?

That damned dentist deserved having his place torn apart.

Pervert. Picking up innocent young women during cleanings. "Yes."

"Well, you can't. You're not invited."

"Damn it, Frannie, next thing you know you'll be telling me you're having lunch at that deli where all the young executives eat. Bad guys don't carry cards or wear signs, you know."

The look on her face said it all.

Drew growled low in his throat. "That does it. You are a menace to yourself. Rick's right. I should just marry you myself. It's the only way you'll be safe. In fact I think that's just what we'll do. We'll get married. There. Search over. But no Ziegfeld Follies or synchronized anything at the ceremony or the reception. I absolutely put my foot down. Justice of the peace, that's it."

Frannie ducked under his arm and batted at his shoulder. "That is probably just about the most insulting proposal any woman, anywhere, any time has ever received." She stomped into the master bedroom, grabbed a pillow off the bed and stomped back to the doorway before shoving the pillow into his chest.

Drew grunted.

"There's your pillow. You wanted the sofa, you can have it. Good night." And she shut the bedroom door in his face.

Drew stood there, staring at the closed door. Banished to the sofa and they weren't even married yet. Of all the—

The door opened. "And Drew?"

"What?"

"Drop dead."

Chapter Ten

Frannie about smothered herself with the pillow she put over her face. But no way was Drew going to hear her crying. "The jerk."

The one thing she'd wanted more than anything since she'd been ten years old had just been handed to her, but he had done it in such a manner that only a woman with absolutely no self respect would take him up on his offer. Scratch offer. Directive was more like it.

This was all Drew's fault.

The jerk.

"Why couldn't he at least pretend that marrying me wasn't the nearest thing to court-ordered community service?" She supposed it was better than a mercy you-know-what, but not much, at least not in Frannie's book. Legalized was about all.

Well, she'd certainly told him. No she hadn't. "Drop dead? That's the best I could do?" Frannie cringed in the bed before toughening her resolve. Frannie tossed off the pillow. Two little words were hardly sufficient. She'd march out there and tell him...and tell him...what?

"Oh, I'm pathetic," she wailed and grabbed the other pillow. She couldn't think of anything evil enough to tell him. Dead was dead, after all. Dead was about as definitive as you could get.

But he deserved worse. The jerk.

She lay there, miserably staring at the darkened ceiling for quite a while before falling into a restless sleep. Frannie woke several times during the night, raising her head to check the digital display on the clock before dropping her head back down on the pillow and determinedly closing her eyes in a parody of sleep until the real thing took back over. She woke for the last time just before six in the morning and decided it was as close to a night's sleep as she was likely to get. The sun had actually been up for a while after all, being as far into June as they were, and if it was good enough for a major stellar body, it was good enough for her.

Frannie rolled out of the bed, almost tumbling onto the floor. "Man, this bed is a train wreck," she mumbled as she untangled the sheets from around her legs. Her head hurt, her shoulders were in knots and she doubted her stomach was going to have much use for any breakfast. "I'm a basket case." She decided to go for an early-morning run to see if she could pound some sense into her body.

Sneaking out the back door so as not to awaken anyone, Frannie retrieved her running stuff from her car where she'd thrown it "just in case."

She donned her shorts and T-shirt, then laced up her shoes. Scant minutes later, she was out running, her legs eating up the street in a steady, satisfying pace. For thirty minutes Frannie maintained her speed, then kicked into her final sprint. Sweat plastered her T-shirt to her back and she was walking through her cool-down when Drew's deep voice hailed her.

"Hey!"

She turned her head. A car she didn't recognize—Drew's sister's?—kept pace with her. "Hay is for horses," Frannie said and kept right on walking.

"Where'd you go?" Drew inquired testily.

Frannie could see the three kids, still in their pajamas but all carefully buckled into belts or car seats in the back seat of the sedan when she gave Drew her you've-got-to-be-kidding-where-do-you-think-I-went? look.

He exploded. "You should have left a note! I didn't know what to think with the bed empty and you nowhere to be found."

"So you immediately assumed that little green men had sneaked in and carried me off?"

Drew was not into reasonableness just then. "They could have! It's possible! It was as likely as any other explanation I could come up with."

"Drew, I'm twenty-four. I no longer have to check in or out."

"Not when you're by yourself at your place, no, but when you're staying with somebody who expects to find you there come morning, yes you do. I couldn't leave the kids alone, so I had to wake them up and everything. You know, basic thoughtfulness doesn't come with an age limit, damn, er, darn it."

He was right and it made her mad all over again. She was the injured one, after all, not him, and she wasn't going to apologize.

Drew evidently recognized that fact, for he sighed and said, "Come on, get in the car. I'll give you a ride back. Now that they're awake I suppose we ought to feed them."

"I need to finish my cool-down."

Drew slapped the steering wheel in frustration. "You are without a doubt the single most irritating female God ever put breath into. Fine. Whatever. I'll see you there. I'll get the kids dressed and fed myself."

She refused to feel guilty. He could just take his short fuse and— Frannie took a deep breath. "I'm walking, not crawling, Drew. It's only a few blocks. I'll be there in plenty of time to help with breakfast." But she stepped up her pace.

And, in fact, she walked in the door to an argument with Chrissie over whether or not she could wear yesterday's clothes again that day.

"They're dirty."

"But they're my favorite."

"They're filthy. You slid in the dirt playing kickball. You dripped ice cream on them. We have to wash them. You can wear them tomorrow."

"Not tomorrow. Today," Chrissie insisted. "We can just brush them off. See?"

"Uncle Drew, I can't find my Blue's Clues shirt. I need it, Uncle Drew. I have to have that shirt. It's my most bestest one of all," Daniel whined.

"Samantha, sweetie, the blue flowers on your shirt are real pretty but they don't really go with the purple polka-dot shorts. We need to change either your top or your bottom. Uh, I don't suppose you know where your shoes are, do you, honey?"

Frannie sighed and entered the fray.

Forty minutes later, Frannie was hoping the children would be less inclined to argue while filling their tummies.

"You pancakes is good, Fwannie."

"Yeah, can I have some more?"

"How come she gots four when I only gotted three?"

"Frannie, I don't like pancakes. You know that. They're too sweet. And did you have to make them with smiley faces? I mean, they're *looking* at me."

Frannie looked at Drew. "And your point?"

Damn. She wasn't going to give him an inch. He took a bite of pancake to placate, but she thumbed her nose at him. That wasn't mirroring. It wasn't even close to mirroring behavior. Drew wasn't too sure what he'd done, but somehow he'd blown it royally last night. He sighed. Frannie had, however, talked Chrissie into wearing a clean outfit and found Daniel a white T-shirt with a blue dog on it that seemed to make him happy. Samantha, however was still wearing blue flowers with purple polka dots. As far as Drew was concerned, two out of three wasn't bad. Not when he'd been batting zero himself.

"Okay, little people, I need you to help your Uncle Drew clean up the kitchen while I shower and get dressed. I've got someplace I've got to go for a little while."

Whoa. The dentist. Not without him, she didn't.

"Are you comin' back, Fwannie?"

"Yeah, are you? We like you, Frannie."

And what was he, chopped liver? "Don't worry, kids, she's coming right back. In fact, why don't we clean up in here real fast while Frannie's getting dressed and we'll go with her? You know, keep her company so she doesn't get lonely at the dentist." Drew smiled evilly. "Maybe you can help the dentist count her teeth."

"Drew—" Frannie began warningly.

"I've got twenty teeth," Chrissie announced. "Ten on the top and ten on the bottom. Wanna see?" She opened her mouth wide.

"Ew, you gots stuff stuck in your teeth, Chrissie," Daniel announced after an interested inspection. "That's gross."

Drew quickly herded the kids out of the kitchen. "Come on, guys. Let's brush our teeth before we do anything else. You're supposed to do that after every meal anyway."

Much against Frannie's will, he drove her to the dentist in his sister's car so Sammie could be properly buckled in.

"I can drive myself."

"This way we can go straight to the beach when you're

done and let them play in the sand for a while. Might as well, we'll be halfway there.''

After half an hour, the receptionist at the dental office asked him to leave, but that was okay, he decided as he let the kids run on the grass out front. He believed the point had been made to that pervert inside that Frannie had attachments and wasn't available.

Frannie built sand castles with the kids at the beach and pretty much ignored Drew. Lake Michigan was feeling testy that day, the water turbulent and cold. It suited her mood. They didn't let the kids go past their ankles. When they got back to the house she settled the kids for a quiet time then sent Drew out to cut the grass while she picked up and vacuumed. Later that afternoon she mixed up a bowl of thick glop with peanut butter, powdered milk and honey and taught the kids how to model bugs with it. They especially liked the flying insects made with almond slices for wings.

"Frannie, you know I don't like peanut butter. Couldn't you have made oatmeal cookies instead?"

He just got one of Frannie's patented you're-such-an-insect-yourself-I-thought-you'd-appreciate-this looks. Her arms were crossed over her chest. She was blocking him, closing him out. Drew was developing a low-grade sense of panic in the pit of his stomach. He'd somehow damaged their relationship just when he'd begun to realize how important it was to him, and he didn't know how to fix it. He'd agreed to marry her, hadn't he? What more could the woman want? God forbid Frannie should ever think anything through, though. Come on, it was all perfectly logical to him. Frannie wanted children. And after this weekend, Drew could see she should have them. She was good with kids, and while it was a woman thing, nesting and all that, it required a little help with the project. Ergo, she needed a man. Drew didn't like the idea of other guys touching her, a prerequisite to having the kids she wanted. Ergo, he'd offered to provide the service. Both their needs were met, the solution clear. At least to Drew.

So what was Frannie's problem?

Ten days later, he got his answer.

"The problem is, you're a complete nincompoop."

This from his best buddy, Frannie's brother Rick whom Drew had met for lunch at a spot halfway between their respective offices.

"Thank you very much, but that doesn't do much to help me solve the problem, whatever it is. Perhaps you'd care to expand your statement a bit. But be careful," Drew warned. "I'm not in the mood to take a lot of garbage from you. Frannie gave me crud all weekend but I don't have to take it from you."

"Frannie's a girl."

"Duh."

"Yeah, duh, moron. They think differently. They're not logical like us. You've got to try and put yourself in their shoes."

Drew was horrified. Think like a girl? "Why would I want to do that?"

Rick rolled his eyes. "Because of the payoff, my man. The payoff."

"The payoff. Right." Drew thought about it. "What payoff?"

"Listen. Why do you think you can't stand the idea of Frannie with another guy?"

"Because they're just after her body. It's just sex for them. Bunch of perverts." And he'd never have thought it of his good buddies at work. It just went to show you never really knew anybody.

"And it's not for you? Just sex, that is?"

"Well, I mean. I—" Drew tried to think but ended up scratching his head in confusion.

Rick pointed his index finger at him. "Exactly. She's hot and you want her for yourself. You can't have her without getting married 'cuz you and I helped raise her better than that so you're willing to put the noose on to get her. Think. What does that tell you, Einstein?"

Drew thought about it for several moments, but came up blank. "What?"

"You are such a 'tard."

"I am not retarded. I simply don't see where you're going with this. I mean, Frannie and I have always been good friends and that's a good thing in a marriage. Once the lust dies out of a relationship that's what's left anyway, if you're lucky. So, why not just start there? It's not such a bad deal if you ask me."

"Well, nobody asked you, did they? And you wouldn't recognize love if it came in and smacked you upside the head. You're in love with her, you moron."

Drew's hand flew to his chest in a gesture meant to protect his heart from further shock. "No! That's not true."

Rick threw up his hands. "Yes, it is."

"You think I— That I—?" Drew shook his head. "No." He continued to shake it in denial. "Just, no." Rick stared at him. Drew finally turned away. "I have to think about this," he said.

Rick responded to his retreating back, "You do that, buddy. You just do that. And when you've done some soul-searching, you just may find the answer to your problem comes clear."

Later that same day, Frannie sat across from Evie at the little laminated plastic kitchen table her sister-in-law had found at an antique mall. Frankly, she didn't think the table was old enough to qualify as an antique, but whatever. It was late Wednesday afternoon, a week and a half had passed since The Weekend. It was miserably hot. She and Evie were guzzling iced tea and the lemon bars Frannie had made the night before and brought with her. Evie had spent the last forty-five minutes describing—in detail—her honeymoon, showing off the wedding pictures, of which there were an insane amount, and expounding at length on all her plans for their apartment.

Frannie picked up yet another lemon bar, took a bite and struggled to pay attention to the monologue.

"...and don't you think it would be cute if—Rick says it's going to look like somebody got sick on the walls but he's a man so what does he know?—I mean, really, don't you agree it would be cute if I splattered paint... All right, Frannie, what gives? Something's the matter. You haven't been listening to a word I've said. What's with you tonight?"

Frannie straightened up in her chair like one of her second-graders caught off task. "No. I've heard every word. Really. Rick got sick. Projectile vomiting I think you said. He hit the wall? That's disgusting."

Evie sighed. "You are totally out of it. Give, woman. Get it off your chest. You'll feel better."

Frannie stared at Evie for several moments, then the floodgates just simply opened and she dumped. Her eyes flowed over while her tongue kept pace and she was exhausted by the time she'd finished her sad tale of woe.

Evie sat back. "Let me see if I have this right. You've loved Rick's friend Drew for over ten years, have I got that part?"

Frannie nodded miserably.

"I kind of suspected something was going on there. So, he asked you to marry him weekend before last and you said no?"

She nodded again and searched through her purse for a tissue.

"Here." Evie handed her a napkin printed with one of those indeterminate designs napkins always seemed to come with. "For God's sake, Frannie, why'd you turn him down?"

"Are you kidding? It was the most insulting marriage proposal in the history of the world!"

"Pffft!" Evie made a flamboyant hand gesture that swept Frannie's statement away. "I doubt that. We have no idea what, for example, Ghengis Khan might have said to his lady love, now do we?"

Frannie leaned forward and jabbed the air between them with her index finger. "Listen to me, Evie. I am not going to settle. I'm worth more than that." Frannie nodded her head in total agreement with her own assessment. "Yes, I am. Look at you. You didn't settle."

"Sure I did."

"You— What?"

"Everybody settles."

"No they don't. They do?"

Evie shrugged, gave a passing thought to calories, then picked up a lemon bar anyway. "Is Rick six-foot-four? I don't think so. Is his salary into six figures? No, although I have hopes for the future. Does he snore? Is he going bald early? Is he incapable of putting the cap back on the toothpaste? Yes, yes and yes."

"But— "

"I'm not done. Is he a steadfast, willing-to-talk-things-through-even-though-you-know-he'd-rather-eat-dirt guy, who loves me to distraction and tries to make sure I know it? You betcha! And that makes up for everything else." Evie looked Frannie right in the eye. "I settled and here's the kicker...so did Rick. He hates that I can be so cheerful in the morning, he doesn't understand how I can stand the ceiling fan on full blast at night and when I start to tell him about something that's happened to me, he gets out a stopwatch. The man's convinced I tell the longest stories in the world. He says I'm physically incapable of getting to the point in anything under ten minutes. It makes him crazy.''

Frannie's mouth hung open. "But...but you guys love each other and Rick's so *romantic* and everything. Remember how he rented the limo for extra time and everything?"

"Yes we do and yes he is. And yes I remember. Those are the very reasons I gave up the idea of reintroducing tall into my children's genetic makeup and am willing to wait for my four-thousand-square-foot house. Now you have to decide what areas of your husband criteria you're willing to compromise on. Drew's a decent height. I think around six feet, isn't he?"

"Um, yeah, I guess."

"Okay, height is good. Shrimpy boys get picked on. He's smart, which is another good thing to pass down to your children. Dumb-bunny children would probably make you nuts, you being a schoolteacher and all. He makes a good salary, is handsome as hell, which improves the possibility for good-looking children, what with you being so visual, and obviously he feels *something* for you or he wouldn't have made the offer in the first place. And, you know, he could *come* to love you. It's not like it's out of the realm of possibility or anything. You're a kind, warm, sensitive person worthy of love."

Frannie sat up. "My point exactly. I deserve better than a toss-away marriage proposal."

Evie put up her hands in surrender. "All I'm saying is that you should give this due consideration. Make a list or something, weigh the pros and cons because you don't want the decision you make now to come back and haunt you in the future. Somebody's going to snap that boy up now that he's finally open to the idea of marriage. It might as well be you.''

''That is so dumb.''

Evie shrugged. ''I chased Rick until he caught me. I'm just saying, think about it.''

''All right, okay, I'll think about it. But I still think it's dumb.''

''Whatever works. If you want him, get him to the altar. Then you can worry about reforming him.''

After that, Frannie went home, where she brooded a lot. That night, Evie confided in Rick. Rick was busy at work, but even so, he managed to get over to see Drew Friday at lunchtime. This time they met at Drew's apartment with Drew providing carry-out burgers from Mickey D's. They munched lukewarm fries while Rick gave Drew the run-down. It was his sacred duty as a friend and an older brother, at least that was how Rick saw it. He told Drew all about Evie and Frannie's conversation. Drew had spent the time—too much time, time he should have spent concentrating at work and sleeping—since their last lunch together in painful self-evaluation. On top of which he was suffering from severe Frannie withdrawal. He'd barely seen her since the weekend at his sister's. That in itself was a real eye-opener. Who'd have thought? He missed the wench. A lot.

''Evie advised Frannie to *settle* for me? Have I got that right? To *settle*? Just because I don't go in for all that stupid, hokey romance garbage?''

''That's about the size of it.'' Rick nodded sagely. Having been married for all of a couple of weeks, he considered himself the resident expert. ''You don't do that junk and they think you don't love them. I'm telling you, big guy, that's the way it is.''

Drew stood, raked a hand back through his hair. ''Man!

What is it with women? What's *wrong* with them? I love her. Why can't she just take my word for it?''

"It's some kind of physiological flaw. They're wired wrong, every last one of them. And since when do you love her? Last I heard you wanted nothing to do with happily ever after.''

Drew shot Rick a frustrated glance. His hair was standing on end now. "I figured it out, okay? I figured it out. I mean, can I have a little credit here? You told me to think things through and I did. It's not like I'm a slow learner or anything. It's not like it's rocket science. I figured it out. I love her, there, I said it out loud. Again.''

"Have you said it out loud *to her* is the question.'' At Drew's killing glare, Rick held up a hand. "All right, all right, let's try a different tack. *You* may be at happily ever after, but as far as Frannie's concerned, well, she's still stuck at the beginning of the fairy tale. She's still sitting in the cinders. You're gonna have to provide the middle chapters.'' Rick frowned at a hangnail on the hand he was examining. "Unless, of course, you want to be the peon she settles for rather than the prince of her dreams.''

By now Drew was pacing the length of his kitchen. It was a small room with many obstacles. The chairs, the table, the cabinets. The exercise only increased his frustration. "She wants a prince? By God, she's going to get herself a prince.'' He pointed a gunlike finger at Rick. "But I'll tell you this, Mr. Smug-as-a-happily-married-bug, anybody laughs, they die.''

Rick put his hands to his chest in an innocent, who-me gesture? "I understand completely,'' he said. "I'm on your side, remember? Besides, I've been there, done that. I'd have shot anybody who gave me a hard time, too.'' Rick gazed speculatively at his best buddy. "So, what're you going to do? Gonna be hard to top me, you know. I mean, I was good, if I do say so myself.''

Drew pinned him to his chair with a disgusted look. He opened his mouth to lambaste Rick. The phone rang. Snatching it up, his snarled, "Hello," sounded more like a curse than a greeting.

"Uh, hello? Drew?" Frannie held the phone away from her ear a couple of inches. Maybe now was not the best time to tell Drew she'd decided to take him up on his offer of marriage. She'd decided to take Evie's advice. She was going to work on seeing this relationship as the proverbial half-filled glass of water. So maybe he didn't love her. It would still be all right. She knew he at least liked her. She'd work hard on seeing their life together as half-full rather than half-empty. Her love for Drew and the children they would produce would be enough. She'd make it be enough. And like Evie'd said, Drew might come to love her. It was possible.

"Frannie?"

Her name came out sounding like an accusation. She swallowed before admitting to the crime. "Yes?"

"I'll see you at seven o'clock tonight, you hear me?"

"Uh—"

"No, make that tomorrow night. Tonight doesn't give me enough time."

Frannie was afraid to ask time for what. She gave a tentative, "Okay. I guess."

Damn right it was okay and no guessing about it. Drew growled, "Fine. Seven o'clock. I'll pick you up. Be ready." He hung up before she could change her mind, then slumped back into the kitchen chair he'd vacated to pace the floor. He scrubbed his face with his hands. "What am I going to do, Rick? Did she call to tell me yes or no? I don't know which would be worse, to have her walk away or to know she was willing to *settle* for me. God, I'm beginning to hate that word." Drew studied the floor between his spread knees.

"It sucks knowing she's loved me all this time and I was too dense to figure it out. And how the hell could it take this long for me to figure out I loved her? I don't know, maybe I am a slow learner, but I'll tell you this much." He lifted his head and gave Rick a stubborn look, a look Rick recognized from long association with Drew.

"What's that, buddy?"

"She is *not* settling for me. Or walking away, either one." Drew hitched his chair in to the table. "Now, here's what I'm thinking."

It was two more weeks before Drew actually kept their date. He'd called her the day after their extremely brief and weird telephone conversation. He wasn't prepared to meet with her yet, he'd informed her. Still too much to do, he'd said, being both brief and weird again. Frannie barely saw him during that time period, which was pretty odd in itself since they were still supposedly working together. Drew had pulled all his crews off their assignments and had spent his days away from the office directing some special project that seemed to be urgent and require absolutely everybody…everybody but Frannie. She was left behind in the office to answer the phone and file.

Every two or three days, Frannie found strange messages on her answering machine when she got home. Not ready yet. Just a few more days, yada, yada, yada.

Ready for what?

And why did Drew only call when he knew she wasn't home?

It was darn strange, was what. Did she really want kids with fifty percent weirdo genes? Maybe she should rethink her answer.

But she loved the jerk. And at least this way she wouldn't have to deal with any mental images of Drew with some other woman. Or that same faceless hussy bearing his babies. No, this was better. Wasn't it?

"I'll pick you up at seven. That should give you time to shower and change into something decent. Oh, and don't eat."

Frannie replayed the message before she erased it. So the man was finally sufficiently prepared, was he? And she was just supposed to fall into line? And wear something decent, meaning he thought she was likely to show up for a dinner date all sweaty and in shortalls and construction boots? Well, she'd show him. Frannie marched back to her bedroom and began ripping things out of her closet to hold them up critically before discarding them into a heap on the bed. She'd find something decent all right. At least by one definition of the word, but by another it would be anything but.

"Ah, here we go," she told herself as she held up a little—stress the *little*—flame-red sundress she'd purchased, then lost the nerve to wear. "This ought to do the trick." Frannie studied the abbreviated skirt and the non-existent back. "Probably freeze to death in the restaurant, but it might be worth it to see Drew's tongue flap."

Frannie clipped the tags from the excuse of a dress and took it into the bathroom with her. She showered, carefully shaved her legs, shampooed and conditioned her hair. She set a personal makeup time record, twenty minutes, the longest ever. No running a brush through her hair and slapping on a little lipstick, not tonight. Tonight there was mascara, eyeliner and shadow. Blush and yes, even foundation. She was going to make Drew sweat no matter how cold the restaurant ran the air-conditioning.

She finished curling her hair as the doorbell rang. Show time.

"Hi, come on. We're late."

That was it? Come on, we're late? Frannie dug in her heels. "Drew—"

"Frannie, don't go getting difficult on me. I've had a bad couple of weeks. Now we're on a tight schedule here, so could you cooperate just a little bit? Geez, it's always the hard way with you, isn't it?"

Drew took her arm and propelled her down the sidewalk to his car. He opened the passenger door and reached inside. "Here," he said. "This is for you."

Frannie took the box of chocolates he handed her.

"You know," Drew said, "chocolate has some of the same chemicals in it that your body releases naturally during sex."

Frannie dropped the box onto the seat of the car as though it was a hot potato. "Is that right?"

"Yes. I did some research."

Frannie picked up the chocolates again and sat down, holding the candy on her lap. "Drew, what's going—"

"And there's more where that came from."

"Uh-huh. Right." Frannie sat quietly, the large box of candy on her lap and watched the streets go by. Drew eventually turned into the high-school parking lot. "Where are we going?"

"Here."

"Here? What for?"

"Patience is a virtue, Frannie. Okay, here we are."

"You keep saying that."

"Come on, out. Our table's waiting."

"What table? What's going on?"

But he said nothing, just helped her from the car then led Frannie across the parking lot towards the football field. "Drew?"

"Shhh." They went through the untended admissions gate, up into the stands and finally way up high into the announcer's box. Frannie came to a halt when she spotted the intimate small round table formally set for two with a white linen cloth and lit taper candles.

"Drew?"

"Sit down, sit down." He made a shooing gesture. "Oh, wait. Sorry. That's right. I have to seat you. Hang on while I pull the chair out for you." With an attempt at courtliness, Drew performed the courtesy.

Frannie looked around her. "Well, this is very—"

"Romantic?" Drew nodded in agreement. "Yeah, I know. And you ain't seen nothin' yet, kid."

Weird might have been closer to her word choice but, hey, the man was trying so Frannie smiled agreeably, picked up her crystal goblet and took a sip of ice water. She cleared her throat. "So, what happens—"

Just then a tuxedoed waiter entered. He had a bottle of champagne which he opened and served with a flourish. A formally attired young woman entered the booth and placed chilled asparagus spears on a bed of lettuce in front of them.

"I didn't know you liked asparagus, Drew."

"I don't. It's supposed to be sexy, though."

"Excuse me?"

"Yeah, you're supposed to pick it up and nibble on the top while looking in my eyes. I'm not sure if it's a phallic symbol or what, but it's supposed to make me crazy."

Frannie's eyebrows raised at that bit of information, but what the heck. She gazed into his eyes and placed the tip of the first spear between her lips. "Umm."

Drew cleared his throat. "Works," was all he said.

By the time a delicious chocolate mousse was served—more chocolate, she noted—Frannie had decided the football arena had no special significance, that Drew just needed a little more practice at being romantic. Who besides a guy would find a stadium romantic, after all? "The mousse is delicious."

Drew gestured with his spoon. "Chocolate. Chemicals."

Nodding, Frannie said, "Yes, I got that. You really gave this meal a lot of thought, didn't you?"

"Damn straight." He cleared his throat. "Chocolate also has caffeine. Keep you from getting a headache. No excuses now."

No headache? Excuses? What? Oh, for crying out... "Would you please explain...what's that?"

Drew frowned, checked his watch. "They're late." He shrugged philosophically. "But we ate slow so I guess it's okay."

Frannie watched kids lugging instruments stream onto the field. "That's the band. What're they doing here?"

"They're marching in the fourth of July parade next week and they have to practice," Drew informed her. "I thought you'd enjoy the concert."

Frannie shook her head. Drew would never be romantic in a conventional sort of way. She should have expected something bizarre if he ever took the notion into his head to try his hand at wooing. And she *was* being wooed, she realized. Frannie laughed out loud. She was charmed. And touched. Drew had gone to a great deal of trouble on her behalf. "This is great," she said. "I used to march back in high school."

"I know," Drew said. "You played flute. I'm not likely to forget what with all the times Rick and I had to run your carpool when your mom was tied up." He scooted his chair closer and took her hand, intertwining their fingers. "Watch."

Is that why he'd chosen this spot? He'd remembered she'd marched in the band? That was kind of sweet, she guessed. She leaned against him, but the meal had not served to relax Drew the way it had her. He was tense against her. "Drew?"

"Here we go," he muttered.

Down on the field, the band started into another formation. Frannie's attention flickered down to the field, then back at Drew. "What's the ma—"

"Watch" she was tersely directed. It seemed important to him, so she did.

"What?"

"Keep your eyes on the field," Drew just about growled, "You're going to miss it!"

"Miss wha—oh my God!" Frannie's gaze shot to Drew. She jumped up, pressed her hands against the announcer's window. "Are they spelling what I think they're spelling?"

"I don't know. What do you think they're spelling?" Drew rose, wrapped his arms around her from behind and rested his chin on the top of her head. "Ziegfeld's out of business, baby, and I have no idea if Esther Williams is even still alive, but I'm trying. I don't think this is a bad substitute, do you?"

Frannie's eyes flooded as she watched the high-school marching band spell out the words, *Will you marry me* with their bodies. It was every bit as good as the Ziegfeld Follies. Better. She sniffed. Drew handed her one of the napkins from the table. "Thanks."

"You're welcome." Drew nodded in the direction of the field. Just when he thought he couldn't feel any more like a fool. "Here come the drum majors."

Sure enough a young man and young woman were running up the stairs, bouquets of helium balloons trailing behind them in a tangled profusion of color. "Did you say yes?" the girl wanted to know as the balloons were handed over. Her eyes rolled. "Like my boyfriend would do anything so romantic. This is like so, not him, you know? You're so lucky. So, did you?"

"Not yet," Drew said. Poor thing. Without *so* or *like,* she'd be unable to talk. Reaching over, he popped one of the balloons.

"Drew!" Frannie protested, then exclaimed, "Oh, Drew," as a red rosebud fell into his hand and was presented to her.

"I found this book. Did you know that flowers have meaning? It's a Victorian English thing."

Frannie grinned up at him. How could she have ever had a doubt? He was too cute for words. And so earnest about this task he'd taken on, even if his face was as red as a sunset. Embarrassed or not, he was seeing it through. "So are you going to tell me what a red rosebud means?"

"Oh. Sorry. Young and beautiful."

Her eyes filled. "Oh, Drew."

He reached up, poked another balloon. Handed her a pink one. "Grace, beauty and gentleness," he said.

"Oh, Drew." Soon she also held a slip of alyssum, a stem of bleeding heart, a calla lily, a sprig of dill, a pansy and a dandelion. It seemed she had worth beyond beauty, Drew was pledging fidelity and she was magnificently beautiful and irresistible. The pansy meant thoughts of loving. Wasn't that the sweetest thing? Her chest felt like bursting. She arched her brow at the dandelion. Was there going to be a weed in their relationship? She was almost afraid to ask. "What's this one?"

Drew cleared his throat. "It means wishes come true. Frannie, my wish is for you to forgive me for anything I've done or not done up 'til now. In return I'll try to make all your wishes come true. Anything you want, sweetheart, anything I can humanly provide."

"Oh, Drew!" Her vocabulary seemed to have whittled itself down to two words. She turned and buried her face in his chest. "I—"

"Not yet." Gently, silencing her with a finger over her lips, Drew spun her out from his chest and grabbed her hand. "Come on. I've got one more thing to show you."

"Wait. What about this last balloon? Shouldn't we pop it?"

"No. Bring it. We're not going to pop that one until we get...where we're going."

He was being high-handed again but Frannie was too happy to care. "Okay." She let him bundle her into the car and tried to be patient as he left the high-school parking lot and the town of St. Joseph behind. Outside the town, the countryside opened up. Drew pulled over to the side of a road by an undeveloped wooded lot.

"What—"

"Not yet. Just another minute."

Frannie sighed but waited for Drew to come around and open the door for her. He seemed determined to provide the perfect evening. She'd be a fool to cut it short, but damn, it was hard. "Bring the balloon," he directed. She grabbed it and let Drew take her other hand. He led her into some trees along a path blazed by some kind of equipment. Back just a ways, the woods opened into a clearing, and in the clearing— "Oh, Drew."

The grip on her hand tightened. She could feel his tension. "You better appreciate this," he muttered more to himself than to Frannie, but she made out the words. "I've made an idiot of myself in front of all the guys to get this done. They're all threatening to quit if you say no. They say I've been impossible to get along with the last couple of weeks."

"You have been."

"No I haven't. That's ridiculous." He erased his words with a hand. "Never mind. You've always been able to make me lose focus. I should have known way back when." He led her into the clearing. In front of Frannie was a beautifully landscaped man-made pond. Several feet offshore a floating platform was anchored. "This is the property I bought for the house I'm going to build some day. Most people do the landscaping last, but I've done it first. For you. Come on." He tugged her hand and brought her to the edge of the pond. Now she could see tree stumps set into the water as stepping stones out to the platform. Drew, in a romantic gesture Frannie would have thought him incapable of just yesterday, swept her up into his arms and took the stepping logs out to the platform before gently setting her back down. "You've got heels on," he explained. "I didn't want you to slip."

"Thank you," Frannie said gravely.

He just looked at her. "Okay," he finally said. "Here goes." Drew gestured around him. "I thought, if you said yes, this would be where we'd get married."

"It's beautiful. I—"

"Not yet." Drew swiped his hand through his hair. "Let me—" He knelt by the edge of the platform, felt with his hand. "Ah, here it is." He must have pressed some kind of switch because little spigots of water arched to life along three sides of the platform, putting the area where they stood right smack dab in the middle of a living water fountain. Drew knee-walked back to her. "Don't laugh."

"I won't."

"You better not. I know you, remember."

"Drew, I won't laugh. I've been trying to say yes for the last—"

"Pop the balloon."

She sighed but obediently pinched the latex surface. What kind of flower was going to appear? What would its significance be? Who cared? She was willing to say yes without anything else, but Drew kept putting her off. It was almost as though he was afraid. The balloon burst. Something gold flashed by, rolled briefly on the platform and plopped into the water.

"What was that?"

"Oh, my God. I knew I'd screw this up."

"Drew?"

"That was the ring. The engagement ring." Drew looked frantic.

"Oh no." Frannie flipped off her heels and jumped over the side of the platform. The water was thigh-deep. She began feeling around with her toes. She'd been waiting too long for this moment, more than half her life, to let it go now. "It can't have gone far."

Drew toed off his shoes and rolled down his socks. "You're going to ruin your dress. Let me."

"We've got to find it, Drew."

He jumped in beside her. "Don't worry." He swallowed hard. "If we can't find it I'll get you another one." That one had been a special order. He'd harassed the jeweler on a daily basis until he had had it in hand.

"I want this one!"

"Okay, okay, settle down." It took twenty minutes, but he'd have stayed there all night if he'd had to. "I think I— yes, here it is, baby. Here it is. God, don't cry."

Frannie dashed at her eyes with the back of her hand. "I'm not crying. I'm not! Oh, forget it. Just let me see."

He dropped it into her open palm.

"How beautiful." The colored stones dripped in her palm, flashed white, blue and green in the moonlight. "Okay, I know better than to think you picked these randomly. A sapphire and what's this, an emerald?"

"Yeah. They're both our birthstones. I—"

"Looked them up," she finished for him, nodding. They winked in her hand. Their birthstones twined with swirls of gold around a forever diamond. "It couldn't be more perfect." She held out her palm. "Here, put it on."

Drew hastily extended his palm under hers. "Careful! Don't let it drop again."

"I won't. I just want you to put it on for me."

Drew carefully took the ring and slid it on the fourth

finger of her left hand. "There," he said with a sigh of relief. They stood in the pond, clothes ruined and soddenly sticking to their bodies. Drew was getting sprayed in the back of the head by one of the fountain spigots he'd so carefully installed. The romantic evening he'd tried so hard to orchestrate for Frannie had turned into a comedy act.

"I'm sorry," he whispered. "But, Frannie? I do love you. I'm sorry it took me so long to figure it out. Don't say no and don't settle. Please? I'll do better."

Frannie looped her arms around his neck and caught the spray that had been hitting the back of his head right in the face. "Oops," she sputtered, turning her face into his neck. He smelled good, she thought. Damp, but all male. "I won't say no and I'm not settling, all right?" She kissed him. "I'm not settling."

Drew kissed her back for a good long while. Finally he released her, hoisted himself up onto the platform then pulled Frannie up. "I've been thinking."

"Uh-oh."

"Seriously." He wrapped his arms around her, although the evening was warm. He just wanted to hold her. Dripping wet, she still turned him on. "You know, September and May, sapphires and emeralds, well, don't you think blue and green would make a nice theme for the wedding? Kind of naturey when you stop and think about it. The blue sky, green grass, me an environmental engineer and all. What do you think?"

"You're just afraid I'll pick pink."

"That, too." He cleared his throat. "Although I'd bear up, Frannie. For you, I'd wear a pink cummerbund and stick a pink hanky in my jacket pocket. For an hour or two."

That's when she knew for absolute positive sure. Drew loved her. And man, did she love him. "Drew? I love you. Whole bunches. Let's go home and dry off."

He squeezed her. ''I love you, too. Let's go home and celebrate.'' He waggled his eyebrows at her in a meaningful way.

They started the celebration in the shower, then dried off and let the party continue for a good long while. Like the rest of their lives.

*   *   *   *   *

Silhouette Books presents a dazzling keepsake
collection featuring two full-length novels by
international bestselling author

DIANA PALMER

Brides To Be

(On sale May 2002)

THE AUSTRALIAN
*Will rugged outback rancher Jonathan Sterling
be roped into marriage?*

HEART OF ICE
*Close proximity sparks a breathtaking attraction between a
feisty young woman and a hardheaded bachelor!*

You'll be swept off your feet by Diana Palmer's BRIDES TO BE.

Don't miss out on this special two-in-one volume, available soon.

*Available only from Silhouette Books
at your favorite retail outlet.*

Silhouette®

Where love comes alive™

Visit Silhouette at www.eHarlequin.com

PSBTB

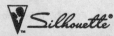

King Philippe has died, leaving no male heirs to ascend the throne. Until his mother announces that a son *may* exist, embarking everyone on a desperate search for...
the missing heir.

Royally Wed
The Missing Heir

Their quest begins March 2002 and continues through June 2002.

On sale March 2002, the emotional
OF ROYAL BLOOD
by Carolyn Zane (SR #1576)

On sale April 2002, the intense
IN PURSUIT OF A PRINCESS
by Donna Clayton (SR #1582)

On sale May 2002, the heartwarming
A PRINCESS IN WAITING
by Carol Grace (SR #1588)

On sale June 2002, the exhilarating
A PRINCE AT LAST!
by Cathie Linz (SR #1594)

Available at your favorite retail outlet.

Silhouette®
Where love comes alive™